"It's just a twinge," Millie protested.
"It'll be fine in a minute."

"I have my doubts," Brig said. "Lie on your stomach and let old Doc McKay's magic fingers do some massagin'." His hands were deliciously strong as he helped her turn over on the bed.

Brig sat down beside her and stifled the groan of pleasure that rose in his throat. She looked so tempting, her blond hair tousled on the pillow, her head turned to one side so he could see her flushed face. He wondered if she would look that way after lovemaking.

He flattened his hands beneath her shoulder blades and stroked down to the top of her shorts, pulling her T-shirt up and enjoying the smoothness of her skin. "Do you know what's best for this kind of muscle strain?" he asked.

"Ice pack," she murmured, barely able to form the words. His touch was mesmerizing.

"Nope. Moist heat." He bent over and placed his damp, hot lips into the curve of her back. Slowly, he slid his mouth up her spine, branding each vertebra with the tip of his tongue. She moaned with pleasure as heat pinked her skin. Nothing had ever felt this good. . . .

WHAT ARE *LOVESWEPT* ROMANCES?

They are stories of true romance and touching emotion. We believe those two very important ingredients are constants in our highly sensual and very believable stories in the *LOVESWEPT* line. Our goal is to give you, the reader, stories of consistently high quality that may sometimes make you laugh, sometimes make you cry, but are always fresh and creative and contain many delightful surprises within their pages.

Most romance fans read an enormous number of books. Those they truly love, they keep. Others may be traded with friends and soon forgotten. We hope that each *LOVESWEPT* romance will be a treasure—a "keeper." We will always try to publish

LOVE STORIES YOU'LL NEVER FORGET
BY AUTHORS YOU'LL ALWAYS REMEMBER

The Editors

LOVESWEPT® • 290

Deborah Smith
Caught by Surprise

 BANTAM BOOKS
TORONTO • NEW YORK • LONDON • SYDNEY • AUCKLAND

CAUGHT BY SURPRISE

A Bantam Book / November 1988

*LOVESWEPT® and the wave device are registered
trademarks of Bantam Books, a division of
Bantam Doubleday Dell Publishing Group, Inc.
Registered in U.S. Patent
and Trademark Office and elsewhere.*

*If you would be interested in receiving protective vinyl
covers for your Loveswept books, please write to this address
for information:*

*Loveswept
Bantam Books
P.O. Box 985
Hicksville, NY 11802*

ISBN 0-553-21942-1

Published simultaneously in the United States and Canada

Bantam Books are published by Bantam Books, a division
of Bantam Doubleday Dell Publishing Group, Inc. Its trademark, consisting of the words "Bantam Books" and the
portrayal of a rooster, is Registered in U.S. Patent and
Trademark Office and in other countries. Marca Registrada.
Bantam Books, 666 Fifth Avenue, New York, New York 10103.

PRINTED IN THE UNITED STATES OF AMERICA

O   0 9 8 7 6 5 4 3 2 1

To the Thursday night group—
Sandra, Marian, and Nancy

One

Millie Surprise had learned to enjoy chaos when she worked for Rucker McClure, the famous newspaper columnist, but that had been two years ago. She was used to serenity now, and the noisy mob of women in the small lobby of the Paradise Springs jail was getting on her nerves.

Hardly anything ever rattled her, so she chalked her restlessness up to the impending arrival of Brig McKay. They'd never had an out-of-state prisoner before, much less a celebrity prisoner. She was going to enjoy fingerprinting a VIP.

"I'm scared," said a wispy voice.

Millie peered over the counter of the receiving desk into the wide eyes of a tiny, auburn-haired girl in a blue sunsuit. The room was packed and she looked as if she might be in danger of being flattened by the restless crowd. "Where's your mom, sweetie?"

"By the door. She told me to wait here. I'm getting squashed."

Millie swung a half-door open, stepped out, picked the little girl up, and sat her on the counter. "How's that?"

"Good." The child eyed Millie's deputy uniform dubiously but smiled after a moment. "You're little," she observed.

"I know," Millie answered drolly, and smiled back. She understood that part of her rapport with children came from her nonthreatening size.

She went back behind the counter and studied the chaos in dismay. The lobby was sleekly modern and tastefully decorated—it hardly looked like the reception area for a jail. The mob hardly looked like a mob either—it was comprised of carefully tanned locals wearing designer sport clothes.

These women should be out playing golf, Millie thought, or shopping in Paradise Springs boutiques. From their style she would have guessed they were fans of artsy New Age music, not Brig McKay's honky-tonk brand of country-western.

A door banged open behind the reception area and the sheriff stuck his head out, a telephone clasped in his hand. Millie smiled ruefully at him. Graying, lanky Raybo Rivers made every effort to be Andy Griffith, folksy and sweet, but his true nature kept getting the best of him. He glowered at the scene in the lobby.

"Millie, what's going on out here? I can barely hear myself think!"

"You said it was okay to let McKay's fans in, because he told his local fan club he'd sign autographs when he got here today."

"I thought he meant four or five people, not half the town! The Nashville courts transferred McKay down here to get him away from publicity!"

She sighed. "I take it that you want me to arm wrestle the cream of Paradise Springs society? That's the only way I'll get these ladies out of here. I don't know what McKay's appeal is, but he sure inspires devotion."

Raybo smiled grimly. "If anyone can whip this crowd into order, you can, Deputy. I'd put you up against a nest of alligators."

"I'll tell these ladies you made that comparison."

"Don't you dare! Get Charlie and Suds on the radio and make sure they're on the way. We'll need 'em."

"Just talked to them, Raybo. Charlie's tied up with another plant theft. Somebody stole four azaleas and a rosebush from a home on South Lakeside. Suds is hunting for two kids who went joyriding in a boat down at the marina." She grinned. "Crime never stops in the big city."

"Then it's just you and me, Millie. Buzz me when McKay gets here. We'll block a path for him."

"Raybo? This guy's not going to get special treatment the whole time he's here, is he?"

"Nah. Just today." Looking suspiciously sheepish, Raybo withdrew and shut his office door.

Millie thought she smelled a rat. Paradise Springs was a small, affluent resort town in Florida's inland lake region. People called it a miniature Beverly Hills. There wasn't much serious crime, and the town council had voted years ago to rent out extra jail space. Raybo obviously liked the idea of hosting this hell-raising entertainer. She made a mental note to ask Raybo's wife if he had any of Brig McKay's albums in his collection of country-western music.

Sighing, she turned toward her counter mate. "What's your name, sweetie?" she asked the little girl.

"Ann."

"Well, Ann, we're the only two girls here who aren't excited about meeting Brig McKay."

Ten minutes later Millie was on the radio with her fellow deputy, Charlie McGown, when the lobby erupted in cheers. "Gotta run, Charlie. Our rebel without a cause will be here any minute."

"Hot damn! I can't wait to meet him."

She was completely surrounded by Brig McKay fans, Millie realized with disgust. She called Raybo on the intercom, then patted Ann on the shoulder. "I don't want you to fall off, hon. Let's find your mom.

Brigand Howser McKay was going to jail. While he knew that he was hardly the first McKay to run amok of the law, he was the first *famous* McKay to do so, and he felt sort of proud about it. He came from a long line of rowdy, independent men and women, and he wanted to uphold the family heritage. He pulled the brim of his battered khaki bush hat low on his forehead, tilted his head back on the seat of the rented Cadillac, and eyed the Florida landscape slipping past.

"Cripes, Chuckie, look at those billabongs over there," he grumbled mildly to the heavyset man in the passenger's seat. Brig took one hand off the steering wheel and pointed out the window. "If I was really keen on bein' eaten by mozzies, this'd be a fantastic place."

"Speak English," his business manager demanded in a rich southern drawl. "Dammit, Brig, I ain't ever gonna figure out your Aussie talk, and I give up tryin' a long time ago."

"I'll translate," Brig said patiently. " 'Look at those lakes over there. If I wanted to be a meal for mozzies— that's *mosquitoes*—this'd be the perfect place.' "

"Florida ain't bad. You'll like it."

"It's bloody hot here in June."

"The jail is air-conditioned, Brig."

"Oughta be gold-plated too. Took a lot of money for the record company's legal eagles to get me transferred here."

"That's the price you pay for privacy—and luxury. As jails go, it's a palace."

Brig chuckled. "I would've been happy with a spot at the big pokey in Nashville. Least I'd be near home. And I like givin' the record company boys indigestion."

"Go easy on 'em, Brig. The promotions people don't get a kick out of seein' one of their biggest names serve time for punchin' a state senator."

"No worries, mate. I'll do my sixty days quietly. Maybe get time off for good behavior."

Brig's business manager grunted in disbelief. "Son, I've knowed you ever since you ambled off the plane from Australia. You wouldn't recognize good behavior if it bit you on the behind."

Brig grinned nonchalantly. "If it looks like a mosquito, I'll just swat it, mate."

• • •

Millie felt a quick draw of breath evaporating from her lungs. The man who climbed out of the Cadillac's front seat wasn't Brig McKay's chauffeur, she knew immediately from the squeals of the crowd behind her.

Brig McKay was everything a man should be, and more.

So this was the womanizer, brawler, tabloid darling, and winner of every major award in country-western music. So this was Brig McKay, about six feet of brawny male perfection in cowboy boots, faded jeans, a white polo shirt, and a wide-brimmed khaki hat that looked as if kangaroos had bounced on it a few times.

He had the rugged, weathered appearance of a man who spent time outdoors doing something a lot more physical than making music. Under the hat she noted a blunt, handsome nose and a droll smile that radiated trouble.

McKay shut the car door with a jaunty slap of one hand, looked up, and stared straight into her eyes. The self-amused smile faded away, and his gaze roamed over her like a heat-seeking missile in search of a target. Millie realized suddenly that her mouth was open in amazement.

Brig thought he'd stopped breathing. After a moment, he covered his heart with one hand and nodded to her solemnly. He felt a thrill of challenge as she stiffened at his melodramatics and her chin went up proudly. Face like an angel, body like a blessing, eyes like a wary tiger, he thought. The combination appealed to him immensely.

"G'day, gorgeous," he called in a deep voice. He swept his hat off, revealing a short-cropped head of wavy, golden brown hair, and bowed low to her. The gesture was both flattering and absurdly teasing. Every woman in the jail thought it was meant for her alone.

Millie staggered as the crowd of female fans shoved past her. She caught the door with one hand and frowned, annoyed that Brig McKay had disrupted her concentration on duty. But she'd never even seen a picture of the man before—how could she have been prepared for a bolt of Australian lightning?

Brig watched as a small child hugged the uniformed woman's legs. The woman reached down and stroked her hair in a soothing, gentle way. That maternal action made a homey and stirring sight to his bachelor's heart. As the colorful crowd of enticing women streamed out of the jail and surrounded him, he put on his most flirtatious smile, but his eyes stayed riveted to the adorable blond deputy. Even if she had been dressed like the others, she would have snared his attention.

A woman stopped beside her at the top of the steps and reached for the little girl. Brig watched as the child blew the deputy a kiss, then turned toward the other woman and said "Hello, Mommy!" So blondie wasn't the mother. Maybe blondie wasn't even married. He realized that he'd been holding his breath.

"I may have copped it sweet here," Brig murmured aloud.

"Oooh, he's talking Australian!" someone yelled.

He dragged his attention away from the deputy as a woman threw her arms around his neck and hugged him. "Easy, doll, I'm breakable," he managed to say, just before she squealed in delight.

Millie grimaced as pandemonium erupted around Brig McKay. Every woman in the crowd seemed determined to touch him, and he seemed determined to let himself be touched.

She was studying him intently when he suddenly looked at her again. It startled her since he was in the process of brushing a platonic kiss on the cheek of a tiny, elderly woman wearing a purple tennis suit. The senior citizen had a wrestling grip on his neck. Brig McKay gave Millie a devilish wink, and it said unmistakably that he had a different kind of kiss in mind for her.

Brig saw her gasp, then frown, then turn to the side and look at the sky and shake her head in disbelief. She had full breasts under the crisp white shirt with emblems and badges of authority on it. Creased, camel-colored slacks neatly encased an athletically-rounded rump and slender legs. Her hair was short, honey-blond, and curly. She looked back at him, one blond eyebrow arched, one hand on her hip, her attitude disgusted.

"Work your way through to his right side!" Raybo called. "I'll get beside him on the left!"

Millie nodded, then angled her way down the steps, prying women aside and feeling short because she *was* short, just an inch over five feet. She ducked her head and peered between bodies as she made her way. Her brother Jeopard had once called her a small blond bulldozer. She'd nearly broken his thumb in retaliation, but he was right.

Mature, sophisticated women were leaping up and down like extras in a bad teenage beach movie. Brig stood languidly in the middle of the action, being pawed by adoring female hands, grinning, signing autographs, and still enjoying himself immensely.

"Deputy sheriff. Let me through," Millie ordered in her gruffest voice. No one listened. Raybo was drowning in a sea of crazed women on the other side of Brig, so it was up to her alone to represent authority and save their prisoner from excessive hero worship. Millie put her head down and aimed for an opening between a pink shorts set and a yellow sundress.

She shoved through, caught her foot on someone's ankle, and gained unexpected momentum in a forward lunge. Her head connected with the center of a hard, flat, nonfemale stomach. The crowd gasped in unison.

"Strewth!" Brig exclaimed in an outrush of air just before he dropped his hat and she slammed him against the side of the Cadillac.

Oh, no, Millie thought desperately. She'd gored the only famous prisoner they'd ever had.

Two strong hands latched into her tossled hair. She was off balance, so she sprawled against his incredibly muscular body, which smelled of denim, leather, and good cologne. Her face was mashed so tightly against his chest that she could feel the mat of curly hair under his shirt.

"Strewth!" he said again. "For such a little Sheila, you scored a wallop!"

His accent was straight from a Paul Hogan commercial for Australia, and combined with his deep voice it was the sexiest sound she'd ever heard. She pushed herself away from his voice and his body, then swallowed hard to regain her dignity in the face of humiliation.

"Sorry, McKay," she said in a raspy voice. "If I hurt you, you can file a complaint."

His hands were still immersed in her hair. She'd knocked the breath out of him, but he wasn't so far gone that he didn't notice that her hair looked like sunshine between his fingers and her eyes were the deep green of new leaves in the spring. He gazed down at her with amused respect at the stern, take-charge tone. "No worries, love. I like this kind of pain."

Love. The nonchalant endearment annoyed her because it was obviously what he called every woman. He let his hands trail slowly through her hair as she stepped back. Lord, the man had eyes bluer than the sky after a rain. His face was expressive and full of good humor, but those eyes held the kind of quiet maturity that comes from years of hard living. She was breathing just as heavily as he was.

"Brig boy, you okay? Y'all ladies get back and give him some breathin' room!" Millie glanced blankly toward the sound of the rolling drawl which sounded as though it were built of grits and molasses. A big redheaded man in a three-piece suit had just gotten out of the Cadillac's passenger side, and now he was trying to make his way through the crowd on this side of the car.

Brig McKay nodded, kept looking down at her, and waved the redhead's concern away with a distracted gesture. "No sweat, pal," he murmured. "I like bein' attacked by little bitty gorgeous women. She couldn't hurt a flea."

Millie smiled grimly and her embarrassment faded.

He was as misinformed about her as most men, and she'd have to set him straight. It was nice to have a package that men admired, but the contents didn't fit their expectations. He stuck out one brawny hand for an introduction.

"Brig McKay, darlin'. Here to sit in your slammer for a couple of months."

She took another step back, pulled a pair of handcuffs from a loop on her belt, and deftly snapped one cuff around his outstretched wrist. For a split second she noticed that it was a terrific wrist, strong-looking and covered in dark brown hair.

"Call me Deputy Surprise," she informed him coolly.

There were shocked mutters in the crowd, but Millie ignored them. Brig McKay might think he was something special, but he was going to be treated just like any other convicted offender as far as she was concerned. His eyes widened with disbelief and he stared down at his shackled hand. Then, to her amazement, he began to chuckle.

At that moment Raybo arrived beside them, and she looked up to find him staring at her bug-eyed. The sheriff was two degrees shy of exploding, she figured.

"There's no need for handcuffs, Deputy Surprise," he said in a low, strained voice. "Unlock that damned thing immediately." He turned toward Brig and introduced himself.

Brig used his free hand to shake hands with the sheriff. Out of the corner of his eye he saw Deputy Surprise—lord, that name suited her to a tee—straighten with rigid pride. She was trying to look ten feet tall, and his respect for her tripled. He hadn't meant to get her into trouble, and he felt bad about it. She faced the sheriff with her head high.

"I overreacted," she said formally, her bearing almost military. "I was wrong." She snapped the cuff off his hand and secured the pair back on her belt without looking, her fingers moving with expert skill. She was a warrior going down with her ship in great honor, and Brig didn't want her to drown on his account.

"I don't expect special treatment," he interjected tactfully. "She was just doin' her job. Guess I oughta get going with this jail term." Groans from the crowd indicated that there were a lot more autographs to be signed. She glanced at him and he read the gratitude in her eyes. Brig knew he'd scored a few points for being a good sport.

"Officially, we don't have to take you into custody until you step inside the jail lobby," Raybo told him. "Stay outside and finish your business, Mr. McKay. No hurry." He glared at Millie. "Deputy, stay here with Mr. McKay. We'll discuss this incident later."

"Yes, sir."

For a second Brig had the feeling that she might salute. He, accustomed to soft and fluffy women, was fascinated by this petite soldier. And charmed. And in big trouble.

She turned toward him stiffly. If her eyes were the color of spring leaves, then a winter storm had just coated the leaves with ice. Her lightly tanned skin was the kind that showed red when she was upset. Man, was she upset right now. "Continue your business, Mr. McKay," she said crisply, as someone thrust a copy of his latest album cover into his hands.

While he signed autographs, Brig squinted one eye at her in a thoughtful way. "You work at the jail full-time, Deputy?"

"Yes."

"Will my life be in your hands?"

"You might say that."

"Is my goose cooked?"

Millie gave him a fiendish little smile. "To a crisp."

He had a cell with a small private bathroom, a window, a plain pine dresser, and brown indoor-outdoor carpeting. He could look out and see the rolling Florida landscape, which included an orange grove and numerous oak trees draped with Spanish moss. Not a bad view, Brig decided, but sure as hell a boring one if he had nothing else to look at for the next two months. He had his guitar and some notepads, so he guessed he'd write about a thousand songs.

Subdued and more depressed than he wanted to admit, he sat on his bunk and peered down at his clothes. A friendly-faced deputy named Suds LaFont had taken his regular clothes and given him standard prisoner duds—a white T-shirt, a white short-sleeved shirt that he wore unbuttoned, and baggy white trousers with a blue stripe on the outside seam of both legs—but allowed him to keep his western boots and bush hat. Brig took one more look at his new clothes.

"I feel like an ice cream delivery man gone bad," he muttered. He lay down on the bunk, pulled his hat over his face, and concentrated on recalling every detail about Deputy Surprise. He fell asleep wondering how the memory of being tackled and handcuffed could be so pleasant.

Millie had new resolve as she walked down the hallway between Paradise Springs' four jail cells. She'd be firm but polite with Brig McKay. This Aussie import wouldn't wreck her dignity again. She stopped in the hallway outside his cell and stared at his lazy, enticing form on the bunk.

The man was a marvel. He gave new meaning to the term *laid-back.*

"Wake up, McKay," she ordered briskly. She put a magnetized card in the cell's electronically controlled lock. The door clicked and slid open.

"Hmmm?"

"Wake up." She walked into the cell, crossed her arms over her chest, and waited patiently. "It's recreation time."

He tilted his head back and looked at her from under the brim of his hat, his eyes sleepy and teasing. "What game do you want to play, love?"

She shook her head in mild disgust and motioned toward the cell door. "We've got a lounge with a TV and a pool table. There's also a fenced-in yard with weight equipment. You can amuse yourself until dinner."

He sat up, swung his long legs off the side of the bunk, and tossed his hat across the room. It landed precisely on the dresser. "Can I stay put? I've got some thinkin' to do."

Millie gave him a puzzled look. "You don't want to sit in this cell all the time, do you? It'll be a long two months."

"Gonna be a long two months no matter how I cut it." He looked toward the window, his jaw set tightly. "I grew up in the outback. During the five years I've lived in the States, I've spent most of my time on the road playin' gigs. I guess I'm used to being about as free as a man can get."

Millie studied the unhappiness in his face, and a traitorous feeling of sympathy lightened her stern attitude. "We'll keep you busy," she told him. "You'll get put on work details, just like any other prisoner."

"I'm the only one in the pokey. Why don't you go arrest somebody to keep me company?"

"Oh, we'll find some other n'er-do-wells to share the jail with you, don't worry."

He turned to look at her, cocked his head to one side, and said in mild accusation, "So, my fine Sheila, you've got no heart for me and think I'm a bad guy."

His Australian accent had a way of turning the end of sentences up, as if he considered everything a question. He talked out of the side of his mouth in a way that she found mesmerizing. For a second she didn't answer, but simply stood there and looked at him. A woman could lose herself in the sturdy contours of that well-lived-in face. Get a grip on yourself, she ordered silently, and took a deep breath.

"Lots of people think you're a bad guy," she informed him. "You attacked a man for no good reason."

"Oh, I had a good reason."

"Hmmm. I'm not going to play judge, McKay. Let's not discuss it any—"

"It was over a woman," he said in a wicked tone. "Everybody knows that. You're just too polite to poke me for information yet."

"I don't care about your love life." It was a lie, but she would never admit *that* to him.

"She was worth fightin' for. Otherwise I wouldn't have walloped that fellow in the Tennessee state senate. Punched him right in the rotunda."

Millie could picture the kind of woman who'd inspire such violence. She'd be tall, tall and delicate. Men didn't beat each other up over short deputy sheriffs. She shook her head to clear away thoughts that were distinctly envious.

"Let's change the subject. The word you said when I, er, rammed you in the stomach—*strewth*—what's that mean?"

"Just a little oath. *God's truth*, shortened. Aussies like to cut sentences down. Saves energy talkin'."

"Why'd you call me Sheila?"

"It's an Aussie word for a prime girl."

"Oh." She frowned at him. "Blarney."

"Blarney?" he echoed.

"Irish word. Means bullfeathers."

"Hmmm." He let the insult pass without comment. "You Irish?"

"Nope."

"I'm part Scotch, meself. Great-great-great-granddaddy was a pure Scotsman."

"How'd he end up in Australia?"

Brig grinned. "Came over on a convict ship."

"How appropriate."

"He was only fourteen. Stole a ham from a fat Englishman, and the English courts sailed him off to the penal colony."

"Hmmm. My great-great-great-grandfather was a pirate. French. He used to attack Spanish ships, and he retired to Paradise Springs after the Spanish ceded Florida to the United States. He was safe here."

"Hurray!" Brig stood up and applauded. "Pirates and convicts! We're a bonzer pair then, love!"

She rubbed her temples wearily. *Bonzer*. She didn't intend to learn a new language from an Australian country-western singer, no matter how virile and intriguing and . . . lord, how her mind wandered when she was around Brig McKay—and he'd only been in Paradise Springs for two hours.

"Bonzer?" she asked.

"It means 'good'. We're a good pair."

She subdued the tingling sensation that remark created. "How do you survive in Nashville with a vocabulary that nobody can understand?"

"They make fun of me, and I make fun of them. It's good sport. And you Yanks love Aussie accents. It's a plus."

"McKay, I'm a sixth-generation Florida native, and most of my relatives fought on the Confederate side of the Civil War. 'Round these parts, you better be careful who you call 'Yank'."

"Oh. Gotcha. I love your accent, Scarlett."

"I love yours—" She stopped as a warning bell went off in her mind. She hadn't intended to get friendly with him, but his eyes stayed on her in a disarming fashion and made her forget her purposes. Millie pointed toward the cell door. "Snap to, McKay."

He ambled toward her, hands on hips, and halted inches from her flushed, stern face. "Where'd you learn to boss people?" he inquired much too politely.

"The navy," she retorted.

Brig gave her a stunned look. "Nah," he said finally. "You're pullin' my leg."

"No, McKay, I was in the navy for several years. Navy police. I've been around. I'm older than I look—I'm twenty-nine."

He was now irrevocably enthralled with Deputy Surprise. She was a buttercup with steel in her blossoms.

Millie gazed up at him grimly. His eyes gleamed with an emotion she couldn't quite analyze, and it made her heart race. She knew that she didn't present the most traditional female image in the world, and some men were put off by it.

Ordinarily she didn't give two hoots what anyone thought of her, but right now she was growing desperately angry because she just *knew* that Brig McKay,

Mr. Aussie Macho, didn't find her background appealing. Her reaction didn't make a damned bit of sense.

"You know, Deputy, I never kissed a navy veteran before," he murmured.

"You never *what*—" she began, just as he bent down and gave her a firm, fast, incredibly skillful kiss on the mouth. He kissed her just long enough to imprint her senses with his taste and scent, drawing her lower lip between her teeth for a nibble. She felt branded.

Millie took a weak step back, gasping for breath and words. By the time she found both necessities, he was already out the cell door, chuckling, his hands in his trouser pockets.

It was going to be an interesting two months.

Two

Millie walked him to the recreation room without another word. She was still stunned.

"A real country club place, this is," he announced with great innocence as he surveyed the big, pleasantly lit room. It was best to act as if nothing had happened, he decided.

"But it's still a jail, Mr. McKay, and there are rules you better follow or you'll be here a lot longer than two months."

He turned to gaze down at her with a contrite expression. His wavy golden brown hair was a little disheveled, and Millie noted that he looked even sexier when he was rumpled.

"I shouldn't have done it, eh?" he admitted. "I know, I shouldn't have kissed you. Now you've got to report me. The sheriff'll probably make me wear a ball and chain around my ankle from now on." His voice rose melodramatically. "It's a price worth payin'. And at least . . ." He sighed grandly. "My lips'll still be free."

"I'm not going to report it," she answered in a cold tone. "I don't want to be laughed at behind my back—and that's exactly what would happen. But if you try it again, I'll defend myself."

"Which means?" he asked.

"Which means, pal, that I'd be perfectly justified to use physical force on a prisoner who threatens me. By the way, I've got a black belt in karate."

His mouth crooked up in a smile. "I wasn't threatenin' you, love, I was testin' your resistance." He shook a finger at her. "I dated a lady wrestler once. I like violent women." He walked to a pool table in the middle of the room. "Want to play?" He cut his eyes at her rakishly.

"I'd beat you, and that would hurt your pride."

He made a clucking noise. "Chicken."

"You may think I'm a joke," she told him coldly, "but I've been a deputy sheriff for almost two years, and I've done a damned fine job of it. I take my work seriously, and you won't get any favors out of me by flirting."

"You know, you'd make a good bodyguard. When I get my walking papers from the slammer, why don't you come to work for me?"

She eyed him speechlessly for a moment, and then she groaned in disgust. "You don't need a bodyguard, you need a keeper."

"Ow." He clutched his chest and looked wounded. "You're the meanest woman I've ever met." And the most irresistible, he added silently. It was crazy, but he was beginning to look forward to the next two months, because he'd be in daily contact with a little Amazon who threatened to beat him up if he kissed her again. Her mouth had been fantastic and more willing than she'd probably care to admit. He planned to kiss her again, and soon.

"I bet you could be a good wrestler," he continued jovially. "I'll put up the money to sponsor you. I'll call you Deputy Death. Or how about the Blond Bruiser?"

"Let's get something straight," she said gruffly.

He watched her intently as she paused. Her eyes were icy but there was something wistful looking about her expression, as if he'd hurt her feelings.

"I'm not delicate and I'm not traditional, but you don't have to treat me like a freak."

He almost winced. How could she so misinterpret his interest? Brig spoke gently. "Love, that's not what I meant."

"Save the sweet talk for your songs, McKay," she answered bluntly. Turning on her heel, she marched toward the door to the cell block.

"Are you leavin' me to rec-reate alone?"

"Get used to it."

After she left the room he leaned against the pool table and stared at the ceiling, pondering ways to learn more about Deputy Surprise.

Millie had the next two days off, so Brig was forced to cultivate sources for information about her. Suds LaFont, her fellow deputy, seemed like the perfect place to start. Suds was an affable young black man who wore wire-rimmed glasses and an air of studious amusement. Suds lived up to his name by providing beer with Brig's dinners, then sat with him in the recreation room while he ate.

"Millie's from a navy family," he told Brig. "No sisters, two brothers, mom died when they were little, father had to haul the kids all over the world to keep the family together. The navy was all she knew. Her brothers enlisted straight out of high school, and so did she. Problem was, the navy's not very good to women. She doesn't talk about it much, but I think she had to put up with a lot of sexual harassment. She got out after a few years."

"What'd she do after that?"

"Went to college at night, worked as a secretary during the day. You've heard of Rucker McClure, the guy who writes that syndicated newspaper column about southern life?"

"Sure," Brig said. "He wrote a nice piece about one of my albums, and I sent him a case of beer."

"Millie worked for him over in Alabama."

"How'd she end up in Paradise Springs?"

"Her father was born and raised here. When he retired, he came back. He died two years ago, and she came down to settle the estate. Decided to stay on. Raybo had an opening for a deputy."

"She ever been married?"

"No. But there was some guy in Alabama. I think he was one of the reasons she didn't go back. You want to know why Raybo hired her? He was really uncertain about hiring a woman, especially such a little one."

"Yes. Why'd Raybo do it?"

"Right after she put in her application, somebody tried to rob her house. She caught the guy and knocked out one of his teeth. Then she tied him up with a garden hose. The guy was an ex-marine. Raybo hired her the next day."

Brig whistled under his breath. What a woman! "She's a regular little Tasmanian devil."

Suds propped his chin on his hands and looked over the rims of his glasses. "May I ask you a nosy question?"

"Sure, mate."

"You're in your mid-thirties, aren't you?"

"Somewhere thereabouts. Mother dropped me off with a tribe of Abos when I was a few days old, and they didn't keep track of dates."

"Abos?" Suds inquired blankly.

"Aborigines. I stayed with 'em about five years, 'till somebody from a sheep station came along and noticed me. Great way to grow up, that."

"What about your father?"

"He went walkabout before I was born. He showed up again when I was ten or so. Grand guy. A little irresponsible, though."

"Good lord," Suds said softly.

"Yeah. Been good to me. Anyhow, what's your nosy question?"

"How come you've never been married?"

"I'm a Tasmanian devil myself, mate."

Suds eyed him with amusement. "Should I warn Millie?"

Brig smiled. "Nah. I think she's already figured it out."

During her two days off, Millie had done little more

than think about Brig McKay. She'd borrowed his albums from Charlie McGown and listened to them all several times. There was nothing delicate about the man and nothing delicate about his music, and both were incredibly sexy.

She'd also gone to the library and looked up old magazine articles on him. And slowly, reluctantly, she realized that she'd misjudged Brig McKay. He wasn't just a troublemaker.

He was a master troublemaker.

In the first year of his career in the States, he and his six-man band played most of the roughest two-bit bars around the country. They got into fights about as often as they made music, but the crowds loved them so much that they invited them back anyway.

His house in the swank, Belle Meade section of Nashville became so notorious for loud parties that the police gave him an award when he moved to a place outside the city. Brig was so pleased by the honor that he donated a huge chunk of money to their union.

Pondering those and other stories about him, Millie waited until he was in the middle of breakfast before she ventured into the recreation room with her cup of coffee. He looked up from a long table in one corner, squinted at her sleepily, then clasped a hand to his heart and stood up.

"Morning, Deputy. I've missed you. My achin' stomach muscles kept remindin' me of our first meetin'."

"I didn't hit you *that* hard."

She sat down across the table from him and watched as he lowered his incredibly well-packed body back into a chair. Even the nondescript inmate's outfit couldn't dim his effect. He picked up a fork and held it poised over a plate of fried eggs and grits. His hands were broad and big-knuckled; it was odd, she thought, that such hands could play a guitar so beautifully. She liked the strength and size of them.

"Did I forget to trim my nails or somethin'?" he asked abruptly.

Millie jerked her gaze up and realized that she'd been staring. "No."

He watched in amusement as the color rose in her cheeks. She pushed her short, loosely curled blond hair back from her face and fanned herself a little.

"It's hot in here," she muttered.

He seared her with a devilish look. "Feels pretty warm to me, too, love."

"Don't call me *love*. It's as bad as *baby* or *honey*."

"You can call *me* love, and I won't mind. Then we'll be even. Or call me by my first name. Everyone else here does."

"I'll call you McKay."

"I'll call you Melisande."

Her lips parted in shock. "Where'd you learn about *that*?"

"Raybo told me."

She took a deep swig of her coffee and arched one brow at him. "I was named after my great-great-great-grandmother. She was married to the pirate. In fact, she was a pirate, too."

"Whew. What a granny. And you take after her, I can tell."

"Hardly. She was very genteel, despite being a pirate. In fact, she wasn't *truly* a pirate—for example, she never killed anyone. But she did sail the seas with great-great-great-grandfather for a couple of years. You see, he helped her escape from Europe when her family was going to make her marry a man she didn't love. Well actually, great-great-great-grandfather *kidnapped* her, because he loved—"

Millie stopped, amazed that Brig McKay had side-tracked her so much that she'd forgotten what he'd said a moment earlier. She thumped her coffee mug down. "You *cannot* call me Melisande," she told him. "No one has ever called me by my full name. I tried to use it once when I was in elementary school, and pretty soon everyone shortened it to *Mel*, and then my brothers started calling me *Mel the Hellion*, so I gave up."

"You're just plain, rough-tough Millie, then?"

Her chin snapped up. "I'm not plain."

Brig chuckled hoarsely. "No, I noticed that the first

two seconds." He also noted that his compliment had just disarmed her anger. She took another sip of coffee and eyed him warily. "You got a fellow?" he asked.

Millie made a soft sound of disbelief. "I won't ask you about the female who provoked you to punch a state senator and you won't ask me about my social life. Got it?"

"You've got no social life, from what I hear," he said cheerfully.

Enough was *enough.* "Finish your breakfast," she said briskly, and stood up. "You've got work to do."

"Oh?"

"We've hired you out to a restaurant owner for the next few days. He pays the city the hourly minimum wage, and you get five dollars a day. I hope you like washing dishes."

"I'll ruin my hands!" Brig said with grand horror. "I'll never play the guitar again!"

Smiling, Millie walked toward the exit, then glanced over her shoulder and drawled, "Bullfeathers."

Raybo opened the door from the other side just as she reached it.

"Melisande!" Brig yelled across the room, "I love it when you talk dirty!"

"*Melisande*?" Raybo inquired. "Talk dirty? What's going on?"

Sighing, Millie slid past him without explaining.

Brig got into the passenger side of the tan and white Paradise Springs patrol car, pulled his bush hat over his eyes, and slept until Millie stopped the car in the parking lot of the Cajun Queen restaurant.

"Cajun Queen?" he mumbled. "In Florida?"

"Paradise Springs is very cosmopolitan. We even have a Siamese restaurant."

"Where the rib roasts are still joined at the ribs?"

She couldn't help laughing. She left him with the manager and promised to come back for him around five o'clock. Brig replayed the memory of her throaty, sweet laughter while he washed dishes.

When she returned late that afternoon, he was sitting cross-legged on the ground outside the restaurant's back door, surrounded by a group that included the day chef, the kitchen assistant, and the owner. They were listening to stories about show business.

"Charmed them, did you?" she asked when he was back in the car.

"No sweat. They could see that I wasn't a yahoo and they gave me a fair go."

"I take it that means you had a good day."

"Yes, my little buttercup."

Millie's lighthearted mood dimmed. "Don't call me that."

"Yes, my little briar," he said sweetly.

She tried to suppress a smile, and failed. He laughed lightly, pleased. Lord, she thought, the man had the warmest, deepest laugh. It reached right down to the center of her body and left a glowing ember of itself. If she put her fingertips against his throat when he laughed, she would feel the vibration. His skin would be slightly coarse, delightfully coarse in a way that was sensual, and she'd stroke a path down his chest. . . .

Millie's languid musings were interrupted when the patrol car rounded a sharp curve and a car shot past, headed in the opposite direction.

"Bloody fool must be doin' about ninety," Brig noted.

"Is your seatbelt fastened tight?"

He didn't even have to ask what she planned to do. "Yes, my little briar," he said calmly as she slammed on the brakes and swung the patrol car around in the middle of the road. The tires squealed as Millie gunned the engine, and she flicked the lights and siren on with a skillfully coordinated movement of one hand. The patrol car zoomed after the offender.

"Good on yer, love!" Brig exclaimed.

"Huh?" she managed, her eyes narrowed in concentration.

"Good work!"

"Thanks."

Brig studied her face as she floored the accelerator.

She had a small, beautifully expressive mouth that could flatten in a line of lethal warning. She had a delicately pointed chin that could jut forward with rigid authority. Her light blond hair curled sexily against the plain, stiff collar of her white shirt.

The contrast of hard and soft in her had never been more evident than at this moment, and Brig realized suddenly that he was sitting in a patrol car, wearing prison clothes, riding along a two-lane road at breakneck speed, and feeling so aroused that he wanted to grin and groan at the same time. It made no sense. Nobody had ever affected him this strongly before, and especially not under such bizarre circumstances.

He was a man of great intuition and quick decisions. He was also a man of quick reactions. That had gotten him into tons of trouble over the years, but just as often had served him well. His feelings for the little blond beauty beside him abruptly crystalized. *Strewth*! Brig thought. This must be *love*. "Melisande!" he said loudly. "I'm falling in love with you!"

She glanced at him askance, then jerked her eyes back to the road. "Did they feed you something odd at the Cajun restaurant?"

Laughing, Brig waved a hand at her jovially. He felt fantastic. "Just drive, Melisande, and I'll explain later!"

They rounded a curve and sighted the speeding car several hundred yards ahead. The road straightened as it entered the rolling green pastureland of a horse farm, one of many in the area. Thoroughbreds were as important as oranges to the economy of this part of Florida. Millie pressed the accelerator harder and the white fences that bordered the road became a blur.

"Sic him, love, run him down!" Brig urged.

What on earth kind of crazy man was Brig McKay? she wondered. He yelled that he was falling in love with her in the middle of a car chase. His hearty sense of adventure seemed closely tuned to her own. Something giddy and companionable rose inside her throat, inspired by his charming nonsense.

"Yeah!" she yelled, and pounded the steering wheel. "I like chasing speeders!"

"That's the spirit, Melisande!"

The patrol car was a few dozen yards away before the other car, a late model luxury sedan, finally began to slow. Within a few seconds it pulled onto the grassy shoulder of the road. Millie parked behind it, turned off the siren, and sighed.

"That bloke gave up too easy," Brig intoned in a solemn voice. "We were just startin' to have fun."

She looked over at him, her green eyes gleaming, her expression sheepish. "It's wrong to enjoy chasing people."

He could tell that she shared his disappointment over the driver's change of heart, but she didn't want to admit it. "The chase is nearly as much fun as the catch," Brig insisted. "It's the same with chasin' women." He lifted one brow rakishly.

She punched him lightly on the arm, grinned, and got out of the car. Brig leaned back in the seat, crossed his arms over his chest, and hummed as he watched her walk to the sedan, which appeared to be occupied by only one person, a man.

A few minutes later when she returned to the patrol car holding the man's license, she was frowning. "Jerk," Millie muttered as she slid into the driver's seat.

Brig straightened. "Is he givin' you trouble?"

"He's a wise-guy kid, nineteen years old, and *huge*. He looks like a bodybuilding fanatic. A Neanderthal. He not only eats Wheaties for breakfast, he eats the box."

"Want me to twist his nose a bit?"

She grinned crookedly. "Get serious."

"Who's kiddin'?"

Shaking her head, she picked up a radio handset and called for a standard check of the sedan's license tag. Several minutes later the report came back—the sedan was stolen.

"This *is* gonna be fun," Brig noted.

Suddenly the teenager shoved his door open. He leaped out, raced across the road, vaulted over the white board fence into the horse pasture, and took off at a run for the forested hills on the pasture's far side.

"Let's see," Millie murmured calmly. "Charlie's on dispatch today. *Charlie*," she called into the radio hand-set. "I'm going to bird dog a six-oh-five on West Grove Road."

"A six-oh-five! Ohmigod!" the other deputy called back. "Ohmigod! Wait there! I'll be there in a minute! No, go on, I'll call Raybo! Wait! I gotta put the bullets in my gun!"

"That bloke does a fair impression of Barney Fife," Brig observed.

Millie nodded. She quickly pushed her door open, reached under the driver's seat, and retrieved a holstered pistol.

"You plan to do a little elephant huntin' with that monster, do you?" he asked. "It's bigger than you are."

"Standard police pistol. I'm an expert with it."

"Puts respect for the law in *me*, love, you can count on it."

"Hah. Don't kid me. You're fearless." She gave him a quick, comic salute. "I'm off, *mate*. Stay here and tell Charlie which way I went."

"Gotcha, sweetheart."

She left the car and trotted across the road, attaching the gun and holster to her belt as she went. Brig waited as she scaled the fence with graceful movements that would have done a gymnast proud. Once in the pasture, she ran like a gazelle. He decided then that the time was ripe to get out of the car and follow her, and he did.

The teenager was muscled, but he wasn't fast. As soon as Millie entered a dense pine tree grove, she spotted him a hundred yards ahead, dodging between tree trunks and slowing down.

She chased him at a lope, keeping one hand on her holstered gun. Once in the navy she'd had to shoot a sailor in the leg. He was belligerent and drunk. He'd trashed a bar near the base. When she and her partner arrived, the sailor broke her partner's arm and came after her with a switchblade. Wounding him was the best option; a completely acceptable one, regardless of her size and gender. Nevertheless, the more pigheaded among the men in the shore patrol had gossiped that only a woman would use a gun in such a situation.

Now she wouldn't pull her gun unless the offender pulled one first. The teenager didn't have a gun, that was obvious.

He was dressed in torn army fatigue pants and a dirty white T-shirt. Millie heard him gasping and cursing as low pine branches snared his face and arms. Moving swiftly and breathing hard, she closed in on him.

"Halt! Sheriff's deputy!" she yelled.

He stumbled to a stop, turned around, assessed her with a smirk, then yelled an obscenity.

"Ouch. My tender ears," Millie muttered under her breath. The teenager continued on his escape route, and she trotted after him. They crested a hill and the pine grove ended unexpectedly at the edge of a steep six-foot drop. His arms flailing, the teenager couldn't stop in time. He flopped out of sight and Millie heard a loud splash.

She slid to a stop at the edge of the drop and looked down on a watering pond. Flat pasture land met the pond on three sides; the hill formed the fourth side. Up to his waist in dark green water, the teenager lumbered toward the pond's edge.

Millie knew that this was the advantage she needed. She holstered her gun, took a deep breath, and jumped in after him.

"Don't you ever give up?" he growled as she landed with a splash and started toward him. His voice shook and he looked at her as if she were an alien creature in the form of a little woman.

"No," she answered flatly, and dove for his waist.

Millie felt a stinging blow as he caught the side of her head with the flat of his hand. She clawed for something to hurt, and luckily found that something in his most tender spot.

He howled with surprise and pain, then shoved her head under water. Millie punched at his legs fiercely, but he had the strength of a bull, and he held her under easily. For one second, she allowed herself to wonder if he intended to drown her.

Then his hands left her suddenly and he fell backward with a violent motion. Sputtering, Millie flung herself upright and gasped for air. Then she gasped again. Brig was standing a few feet away from her, soaking wet, his hands on his hips. The teenager was gone.

"Where is he?" she demanded breathlessly.

Brig shifted as if he had trouble keeping his balance. "He's eatin' mud."

"*What*?"

"It's an old aborigine trick. I'm standin' on his head. Takes just the right technique, you see, otherwise he can get up."

She realized abruptly that the water was churning around Brig. "Don't drown him!"

"Aw, I'm just havin' a bit of fun with him."

He stepped back and the teenager rose slowly to the surface. The parts of his face that weren't covered in sticky pond mud were a robin's egg shade of blue. He slumped over and braced his hands on his knees, heaving as he caught his breath. Millie saw the look change in Brig's gaze. He eyed the huge teenager with quiet, icy fierceness. The jovial, carefree McKay had another side—a deadly one.

"Make a move, you mangy baby, and I'll rearrange your face," he said in a soft tone. "If you've got a notion to hold somebody else under water, give it a go with me instead of the lady."

"No, no." The teenager could barely stand up. "Forget it."

Millie wasn't accustomed to being defended, and she should have bristled at Brig McKay's insinuation that she needed protection. Instead, she smiled at him until her lips hurt. He was wonderful.

"I knew you didn't need much help," Brig told her

gallantly. "But I figured you'd be out of breath by the time you finished chewing his legs off under water."

Millie pulled the teenager's hands behind his back and cuffed them. Her eyes hardly left Brig's. "You hellion," she said without much malice. "You were supposed to stay in the car."

The gaze he gave her was so possessive that she lost what little remained of her train of thought. She read a proud message in his blue eyes: He'd never intended to let her chase a car thief alone.

"You look real good, even wet and dirty," he told her.

"Oh, God, I don't believe this," the teenager muttered. She guided him to the bank and he sat down limply. "Is this a bad episode of *Charlie's Angels*? A little chick tries to tear my family jewels off, her English friend nearly drowns me, and now the two of them are tryin' to start a romance."

"Shut up, yahoo," Brig told him grimly. "I'm not English, I'm Australian, and don't forget it. Watch your trap or I'll sic the lady on you again."

The teenager groaned. "Anything but that, man."

"Make one wrong move," Millie added, "and the *Englishman* will use another aborigine trick on you."

She looked at Brig while her chest swelled with affection and respect and something much more intense that, were she not a serious, practical, rough-and-tough deputy sheriff type, she would have called love.

Three

The car thief was wanted by the police in the neighboring county, and within an hour of his arrival at the Paradise Springs jail, officers from that county came and got him. By the time Brig cleaned up and changed into a dry set of jail whites, Millie had left for the day.

Feeling disgruntled because she didn't bother to say goodnight—after all, he had stopped that ape from drowning her—Brig sat on his bunk and stared out the window, remembering how she'd smiled at him.

There had been many women in his life, not nearly as many as everyone thought, but nonetheless a lot, and the fact that he couldn't settle down bothered him. Something had never clicked, something had always kept telling him to move on. Until now. Now an intuitive sense told him that he'd never find anyone else like Melisande Surprise.

He felt both peaceful and restless, and groaned in dismay. This had to be love—he was as confused as a stunned mullet.

The sound of someone coming down the hall made him look around. Charlie McGown was *big*, a human tractor with red hair and a paunch. His size and the accompanying strength it gave him were the only things that made him dangerous. He was as violent as a daisy.

"Hi ya, Gowy, how's it goin'?"

Charlie grinned at him. "Raybo says from now on you can come and go as you please. Inside the jail, that is." His huge hands fumbling with the small magnetic card, Charlie unlocked the door to Brig's cell. "You earned some privileges after what you did for Millie today."

"Thanks, mate."

Brig went to a corner and got his guitar, then sat back down on the bunk.

"Aren't you comin' out, Brig?"

"Nah. I got a song to write. If I don't get it out into the air, it'll stick in my craw all night."

"Sounds like a bad case of indigestion to me."

Brig chuckled ruefully. Melisande Surprise was a lot worse than indigestion—she was disturbing all the way down to his bone marrow. After Charlie left, he leaned against the wall, closed his eyes, and tried to sort out his emotions. Would writing a song make his heated feelings of disappointment and arousal fade away? Hell, no, he decided, but it was the best alternative he had.

An hour later he had gotten the melody and most of the lyrics roughed out. Music had always come easily to him, even as a youngster. He'd honed his skills in rough outback pubs where his guitar was a handy weapon as well as a musical instrument. Because of those years he could concentrate on his music no matter where he was or what was going on around him.

Millie heard his rich baritone voice as soon as she opened the door between the reception area and the cell block. She halted, charmed. His albums couldn't capture the raw magic.

"Wiiiild woman," he sang heartily. "Tearin' at my heart, tearin' me apart, then you put me back together with a sweet look or two, watch your step, baby, cause I'm just as wild as you."

The challenge in his tone made her shiver. He *was* wild, and she was drawn to him like a tiger looking for a mate. But who was the inspiration for his lyrics? Not herself, certainly. Men didn't write love songs about her kind of wildness. They wrote about the bedroom kind, not the kind that made a woman dive after car thieves in muddy ponds.

Millie went to the cell door and looked in at him. He strummed his guitar and rested his head against the wall behind him, his eyes closed. What woman provoked such reverie? she wondered. The one back in Nashville? "Nice music," she announced bluntly.

"Melisande!" His exuberant shout nearly made her jump. She stepped back uncertainly as he leaped up and trotted to the door. He slid it open and stared at her happily, his blue eyes gleaming. "I've never seen you without your clothes on before!" She looked at him in consternation. "Without your uniform," he corrected.

Millie resisted the urge to shift from one foot to the other as he studied her white shirtwaist dress and white sandals. She'd chosen the outfit because it didn't look provocative. She certainly didn't want him to think that she was deliberately dressing up for him. But he was looking at her as if she were wearing a gown that was paper-thin and low-cut. Millie fanned her face with one hand. Damn the man—he made her overheat everytime she got around him.

"I brought your dinner," she told him. "It's special, in honor of your help today."

Brig glanced eagerly at the medium-sized ice chest she held by her side. "I thought you'd gone home for the night."

"I wanted to surprise you," she said. "Surprises sort of suit me, don't you think?" She nodded toward the door to the reception area. "Want to go outside? We've got a picnic table under one of the trees."

I'd go anywhere with you, Melisande. He didn't say it, figuring that subtlety was called for at the moment. "Sure."

They walked through the lobby, where Charlie sat behind the counter with his feet propped on a desk. Outside, the shadows of a summer evening were teasing the oak trees, and the neat lawn around the jail smelled of a fresh mowing. Crickets sang in the hardwood grove on the other side of the quiet little road that fronted the jail.

"This is a lot better than eatin' in the rec room," Brig commented.

Millie put the cooler on a redwood table under one of the giant oaks that bordered the parking lot. Brig sat down and watched in fascination as she set out a pan of lasagna, a large bowl of salad, garlic bread, and finally, several oversized cans of Australian beer.

"This is sweet, Melisande. You're a bobby-dazzler."

"Is that good?"

"Very good," he said seriously. They shared a long, intense gaze until she looked away and shoved a can of beer toward him.

"It's just a celebration dinner," she told him almost defensively.

"Celebratin' what?"

"My being undrowned. Your being stubborn and heroic."

He chuckled. "Sit down and eat, my little briar, and let's talk about naughty things."

Millie sighed grandly. "What *else* would I expect to talk about with you?"

But they discussed many things, most of them not particularly naughty, some of them downright homey. She told him that she had a large collection of record albums, including some country-western, but that her musical expertise was limited to a lengthy high school association with a clarinet.

He grinned at that. "Why a clarinet?"

"Because Dad was in the navy, and we moved almost every year. Bands can always use one more clarinet player. Made it easier for me, as a new kid, to get involved."

"You must have been pretty lonely sometimes, movin' from place to place."

She nodded. "It either makes a child extremely shy or extremely self-sufficient. I managed the latter."

"I bet you were one tough clarinet player."

She grinned. "You got it."

Brig fascinated her with information about the inner workings of the record business, and she realized quickly that he was as much an expert businessman as he was a free spirit. Then he told her stories about the town where he grew up, a place where sheep stampedes were the main source of entertainment.

"And what was the name of this exciting place?" she asked.

He smiled slowly. "Washaway Loo." When she looked puzzled, he explained, "A spring flood carried off half the outdoor plumbin' facilities one year."

She laughed until she began to hiccup. He handed her his can of beer and it was so big that she had to put both hands around it to lift it to her mouth.

"You got pretty little paws for such a violent lady," he told her. "Lethal little paws."

It was an odd comment, but he made it so sincerely and with such admiration that she nearly started hiccupping again. When she regained her composure and set the beer can down, she found his warm, magnetic gaze on her face.

Millie took a deep breath. Now was the time to say what had been on her mind for hours. "You like to tease me, and that's all right," she told him solemnly. "It's fun—I admit it—but don't say things like you said in the car today."

"What?"

She arched one blond brow at him. " 'I'm falling in love with you, Melisande.' That's going too far."

"Maybe it's the truth."

Millie stared at him for a moment. "Maybe it's a line," she said quietly.

"Sounds like one, that's for sure," he agreed, nodding his head. Then he focused a searing look on her and added, "But it's not."

She clasped her hands in her lap and tried not to appear as stunned as she felt. "We met four days ago. I butted you in the stomach and put a handcuff on you. I don't think that's a sign of compatibility."

"I'm just gonna have to convince you that you're my kind of Sheila."

She began to get angry. "Any Sheila will do under the circumstances. You're a captive audience."

"Think poorly of yourself, do you?"

"No," she retorted. "But I've read all about *you*. You go through women like water through a sieve."

"I have my picture taken with a lot of women. I didn't know that meant I was toyin' with 'em all." He paused, looking perturbed. "If I'm havin' that much fun, I oughta take vitamins."

Millie shook her head wearily. She propped both elbows on the table and planted her chin in her hands. "Brig," she murmured. "Short for *Brigand*. The dictionary defines brigand as *bandit*."

"And a wallopin' good name it is, too, Melisande."

"*Stop* calling me Melisande! People will laugh at me!"

He suddenly moved around to her side of the table, sat down beside her on the bench, and pulled her hands away from her face. He held both hands tightly, his fingers buried in the warm hollows of her palms. Millie met his eyes and found no more levity in them. He looked almost angry.

"You've got an image problem," Brig told her tautly. "You don't see anything delicate or elegant about yourself, but that's because you're blind. I see it—the fineness."

She could barely speak. "You . . . you're crazy."

"And you like it."

Millie couldn't deny *that*, and he didn't give her a chance. He bent his head and kissed her hard, breaking through her barriers in the quickest and most intimate way he knew.

Anger warred with confusion inside Millie's mind, and both were overwhelmed by the incredible sensation of his mouth on hers. She pulled back. He pushed forward, capturing her lips again and making a gruff sound of reproach as he did.

Millie responded with a huffing sound of rejection, but by then her lips had parted without her cooperation to allow the hungry surge of his tongue. Why hadn't anyone warned her that Australian men kissed better than anyone else on earth? And that Brig McKay was the best of the best? He smelled soapy clean and enticingly masculine. His fingers stroked her palms in a way that promised similar attention to the rest of her body.

Brig twisted his mouth gently, and a thrill shot through him as he confirmed that she wanted him to kiss her as badly as he wanted her to kiss him. Suddenly, almost as if to prove that she could match him, she jerked her hands away from his and grasped his face.

Her mouth devastated him with a take-charge series of capricious movements. She licked his lower lip, kissed the corners of his mouth, then lifted her lips to the tip of his nose and kissed it. A second later she was taking his mouth again, and he thought he'd die from wanting her. This passion went beyond simple satisfaction into a whole new realm of need. If he tried hard enough, he could draw this feisty, beautiful little woman into his soul and absorb all her courage and strength.

Millie pulled back from him quickly and they stared at each other, both breathing hard. "You're a prisoner here and I'm a deputy!" she exclaimed guiltily. She put one hand to her forehead and groaned. "This is terrible. I just violated my duty."

"Violate it some more," he urged, and leaned toward her.

She put both hands on his chest and held him back. "Don't kiss me again."

"But that won't keep you from kissing me first, will it?"

"I can control myself."

"We'll see about *that*, Melisande."

Challenge radiated between them in the silence that followed. They stared into each other's eyes, reading the recklessness there, and Brig knew that she was on the verge of kissing him again.

Slowly, one of her arms rose, and her hand balled into a fist. She didn't look angry, she looked desperate.

"You gonna whack me?" he asked in a husky voice.

She blinked rapidly, dropped her fist into her lap, and shook her head. Smiling tautly, he got up and went back to his side of the table. Brig gestured toward her unfinished plate of lasagna. "Better eat, or you'll have to heat it up."

Millie glanced down at the food and thought numbly that nothing around her and Brig *needed* heating up.

"Aaaall I need is a little chance with you," Brig sang under his breath. He paused to fork another load of fouled straw into the wheelbarrow outside the horse stall. "A little time to show that I'm true . . . truuue. Nah. Blue. Nah. A little time to show that I kneeew. Augggh! *Strewth*!" The woman had fuddled his mind until he couldn't rhyme.

He'd hardly seen his Melisande in the past four days, since the city had hired him out as a stable hand at Paradise Farms, a multi-million dollar Thoroughbred operation. She made certain that Suds or Charlie transported him to and from the farm, and she made certain that she wasn't around when he returned to the jail each evening. Brig made a one-word comment on the situation, then looked at what he was removing from the stall and smiled sardonically. "Perfect," he muttered.

Every day he tried to work out his frustration through hard physical labor, but still he lay awake at night, thinking about her, his body tight and his mind full of plans. He had his tactics outlined now. Over the next few weeks Melisande Surprise was going to get more temptation than she'd ever imagined possible. By the time he became a free man again and she had no more reason to hide behind her deputy's badge, she'd be ready to follow him anywhere.

"Aaall I need is a chance with you," he tried again, jabbing his pitchfork into a pile as he sang. "You took my heart and made it new. Run with me into the night, capure the stars and . . . *I'll give you the light.*" Brig cursed darkly and shook his head. "Sounds like I'm offerin' to fire up her cigarette!"

It was hopeless. Melisande would simply have to fall in love with him, or he'd never again come up with a proper rhyme.

As Millie brought her old Buick to a stop in the stable yard at Paradise Farms, John Washington, the stable manager, was already on his way to her door. "Howdy, neighbor," he said cheerfully. "Saw you comin' up the driveway like a juiced bobcat." He took a long look at her sweaty face and disheveled hair. "Anything wrong?"

"A tree fell through my roof." The Buick was one of the last of the dinosaur convertibles. She had the top down, so instead of getting out, she simply climbed over the side. Millie leaned against the door, crossed her arms over her chest, and sighed wearily. "At least it happened on my day off."

John flashed ivory-white teeth in a face the color of dark chocolate. "Aren't you lucky?"

"I was just wondering if you could spare someone to help me move the tree and fix the roof. I'll pay."

He ran a hand over his stubbly, graying hair and looked sympathetic. "No can do, Millie. I'm short-handed—that's why I hired your fancy prisoner."

"How's my Aussie singer doing?"

"Shovels like a pro, doesn't expect special treatment, tells good dirty jokes. Hey, why don't you take him over to your place to work on the roof? If Raybo doesn't mind, that is."

"No. Oh, no," she said quickly, raising both hands in a gesture of defense. "I'd rather have a permanent sky-light than—"

A whistle pierced the air. They both turned toward the wide hallway of the farm's main barn. Millie watched dolefully as Brig ambled toward her, a pitchfork balanced on one shoulder, a plastic cup in one hand. His white pants were so sweaty that they clung to his thighs in an intriguing way. The white T-shirt he wore was molded to his damp chest, outlining solid muscles and wide shoulders. His wavy hair was ruffled.

I know my control's shaky, Millie thought raggedly, because this is the first time I've hyperventilated at the sight of a man who's been cleaning stalls all day. She concentrated on breathing and squinted at him warily.

"I'm takin' my water break, John," Brig told the stable manager cheerfully. "If that's okay with you, mate."

"Sure."

"G'day, Deputy. Come by to check me out?" His eyes roamed approvingly over her pink T-shirt, cutoff jeans, and jogging shoes, and he whistled under his breath. "I *like* your new uniform."

"I'm off work today. I live near this farm."

"And a tree fell on her roof," John interjected.

Brig arched one brow and gave her a mischievous look. "Practicin' karate on it, were you?"

"It's a very old oak and it has a root disease. I'd been planning to have it cut down, but I obviously waited too long."

"And she needs a handyman to help her move it," John added. "You're almost done here for the day. It's okay with me if you want to go with Millie."

"No!" she said. "I'll call a tree service."

"Melisande, I'll cost you a lot less than a tree service," Brig said innocently. "Don't you want to let a humble prisoner pay off some of his debt to society?"

"You couldn't get a tree service to send anyone out this afternoon," John said. "And you need to get some kind of cover over the hole in your roof. What if it rains tonight?"

Millie looked up at billowy white clouds in a blue sky. "Unlikely." She sighed. "But possible." She hesitated, then put reluctance aside and muttered, "I'll call Raybo and ask him what he thinks."

"About the weather?" Brig asked coyly.

"About me hiring you to work on my roof."

"How much will you pay me, love?"

"It's the same deal no matter who you work for."

"But this is special. I might have to do things I wouldn't do for anyone else."

"Wrestle an oak tree?" Millie glanced at John and found him grinning widely. Suddenly she realized that anyone with eyes could see what was going on between her and Brig. She stiffened and frowned. "Can I use your phone, John?"

"Go right ahead, Millie. There's one inside the barn entrance. Left side."

"I'll be waitin' in the car, Melisande," Brig added.

"Melisande?" John echoed in an incredulous voice. Then he laughed heartily. "She's not a fancy *Melisande*, boy. She's little ol' Millie, the toughest female this side of the Mississippi."

Millie felt color rising in her cheeks. It didn't matter that Brig gave her an apologetic look as she marched past him toward the barn. He was in deep trouble.

"Look, sweetheart, I don't know sign language, and I've taken a likin' to the sound of your voice."

Millie cut the Buick's engine and shoved her door open before she glared at him. "This is my home," she said sharply, and swept her hand toward a whitewashed cottage surrounded by colorful flower gardens and huge trees. One of the trees hugged the back corner of the gray-shingled roof. "That's the tree. There's a shed in the backyard where you'll find tools and a ladder. I'm going inside to get my work gloves. I might have an extra pair that will fit your big hands, but if I don't, I'll enjoy watching you get blisters."

"Ow. That's cold." Brig stood, grasped the passenger door, and vaulted out of the car with a fluid, athletic movement. He watched quietly, feeling troubled, as she went inside without another word, then turned his attention to his surroundings. Her house sat at the end of a long, graveled driveway in the midst of an old, old forest. It was a lovely place but somehow strange.

He finally determined why. The telephone and electrical lines were underground. Except for the car's presence and the asphalt roof shingles, he might have been looking back through time at least a hundred years.

Brig was inside the backyard shed when she brought him a pair of gloves. "Here, McKay," she ordered, and thrust them at him.

Without looking up from a box full of carpentry tools, he replied in a low, firm voice, "Use my first name or it's no go."

"I don't have the time or the patience to argue with you. All right. Here, *Brig*."

He took the gloves, then looked her straight in the eyes. "And be civil to me. I'm sorry John Washington laughed at your name, but I'm still gonna call you Melisande, because I like it and it suits you. And if you thought of yourself as a Melisande, pretty soon other people would too."

This aura of cool authority was a new angle to his personality, one that made her gaze back at him speechlessly. "Call me what you like," she finally managed to say. "I've given up trying to get your cooperation."

"You've got my cooperation. And my respect, *and* my friendship. Quit treatin' me like a croc who's about to gobble you alive."

"Quit flirting with me then."

"Melisande, m'dear, flirtin' is ingrained in my nature. But that doesn't mean I'm an Ocker gone troppo."

"*A what?*"

He rubbed his head and thought for a moment. "A daffy redneck. I'm not gonna pounce on you like a kangaroo with an itch." He paused. "Not right away, at least."

"That's very reassuring," she said dryly. Under her T-shirt her heart was racing. Just when *did* he plan to pounce on her? And what would she do about it? He was a prisoner and she was a law officer. She'd never forget that barrier. And she wasn't his kind of woman—she didn't know whose kind of woman she was, anymore—but one thing was certain. She wasn't going to get involved with a man who'd eventually leave Paradise Springs without looking back.

"Can we get to work?" she asked bluntly.

He smiled and looked at her through slitted, reproachful eyes. "*Please.*"

"Can we get to work, *please*, your Australian highness?"

"Righto, love."

They carried both hand and chain saws to the side of the house. Brig nestled the ladder between two enormous crepe myrtle bushes by the wall, bowed low, and swung a hand toward it. "You first, Melisande. I'll catch you if you try to fly."

She curtsied, then climbed to the roof without faltering. Brig stood below and admired her beautiful round rump without the least bit of pretense. Millie knew it, and couldn't manage to feel anything but giddy. When she reached the roof, she sat down and fanned herself furiously.

Holding the hand saw, Brig climbed up beside her, then pulled the chain saw up with a rope before getting lithely to his feet and picking his way through the tangle of tree limbs to the point where the trunk had torn a hole in the roof. Millie followed carefully and stood beside him, gazing down.

"Glory be," he said in an awed tone. He bent over and braced his hands on both knees, all the time gazing at the gash in the roof. "This tells me what to expect. It's gonna be interestin'."

"Is it so bad that it can't be fixed?" she asked weakly. "Do you think I'll have to replace the whole roof?"

"Pink satin. You've got pink satin sheets. I can see 'em on your bed."

He began chuckling even before she slapped his shoulder and sputtered, "Concentrate on the roof, buster." But when he turned to look at her, his expression was so affectionate that she smiled at him.

"You've got a fantastic smile, Melisande." He became

brusque with comical suddenness. "But no more of *that* kind of kookaburra chatterin'. You use the hand saw and I'll take the chain saw. Love, have you *ever* used the chain saw? It probably weighs more than you do."

"It belonged to my father. I admit defeat where it's concerned. I managed to crank the thing once, and I nearly cut off my toes. I'll be happy to stick with the hand saw, thank you."

"Well, then, let's start attackin' the limbs on this mangy hunk of tree."

They worked for nearly an hour before the chain saw ran out of gas. Even in early evening the sun was scorching, and they sat down on a corner of the roof that was shaded by another large oak. Brig pulled his shirt off, wiped his face briskly, then handed the shirt to her.

Millie allowed herself a couple of heart-stopping seconds to admire his naked, hairy chest, and then she rubbed her face with his T-shirt as if she could erase his appeal from her mind. She chose the wrong avenue for escape, because his shirt carried his scent and the erotic dampness of his sweat. She handed it back to him and tried to arrange a neutral expression on her face.

Brig tossed the shirt aside and lay down on his back with his arms under his head. Millie thought that laying down beside him would be the most thrilling and also the most dangerous thing in the world—even on the roof—so she remained upright.

"What a homeplace this is," he murmured, gazing up at the oak tree's massive limbs. "How old is it?"

"Over a hundred and fifty years. You remember my great-great-great-grandparents, the pirates?"

"Hmmm."

"This cottage was their first home. It was built in 1835. They owned hundreds of acres around it. They built a manor house about half a mile from here, but after they died it got in bad condition. One of their great-grandchildren inherited it, and he burned it down."

"And what's become of all the land?"

"It was parceled out to various relatives, who sold it bit by bit. Now this cottage and a few acres around it are all that still belong to a member of the Surprise family. It's all that's left of the old Surprise plantation."

"Plantation? Why, Scarlett! What an interestin' family you have!"

"It wasn't something out of *Gone With the Wind*. It was more like the wild west, especially during the wars with the Seminole Indians. Plus, my family never owned slaves."

"Good for them," he said sincerely. "A bonzer heritage you've got, love."

She had to think for a moment to recall that *bonzer* meant something good. "Thank you."

"And how did a French pirate get a name like Surprise?"

She chuckled. "His name was Jacques St. Serpris. He Americanized it to *Surprise*. I think great-great-great-grandfather had a sense of humor. I know he was stubborn."

"Eh?"

"This cottage is built of coquina. It's a sand, shell, and mortar mixture that's as sturdy as modern concrete. But the ingredients had to be hauled all the way from the coast. According to an old diary left by great-great-great-grandmother Melisande, Jacques was determined that their honeymoon cottage would never be destroyed. It's survived Indian attacks, tornados, and fires. Believe me, the roof may fall in, but the walls will always be here."

"Old Jacques was a romantic. I think I like him. You said something once about him kidnappin' Granny Melisande?"

"Uh-huh. Stole her right out of her bedroom the night before her wedding to a minor member of the Spanish royalty. I think she was thrilled to escape the marriage, but not so thrilled to be carried off by a pirate." Millie smiled. "Obviously, at some point, she changed her mind. They had eight children."

"So, my little Melisande, are you waitin' to be carried off by your own pirate?"

Millie's smile faded. "Pirates carry off damsels in distress, not deputy sheriffs who know karate. I don't believe in fantasy."

Brig rolled over on one side and propped his head on his hand. He eyed her shrewdly. "You had a special bloke back in Alabama, when you worked as a secretary for Rucker McClure. Suds told me."

She arched one brow and gave him a sardonic look. "Remind me to thank Suds."

Brig's voice was gentle. "You got your heart trampled. I can tell."

She nodded. Oddly, she felt comfortable talking to Brig about it. Later, she'd have to analyze this strange turn of events. "After two years of devoted fantasy, I 'got my heart trampled'."

"You were too much woman for him."

"Thank you. I wasn't enough woman for him. Not in the ways that men think are important."

"What men?" Brig asked bluntly. "Don't go lumpin' us all together like grits in a tub."

She smiled, and suddenly she realized how easy it was to adore him. Millie shoved that worrisome thought aside. "Grits don't lump if you cook them right," she corrected.

"Don't change the subject. I'm itchin' to know what us men want from women."

Millie forced herself to look nonchalant. "Oh, you want a combination of Marilyn Monroe and Betty Crocker."

"Who's Betty Crocker?"

She kept forgetting that he'd only been in the States a few years. "Never mind. The point is, men don't know how to react to women who act macho."

"Well, Rambo Surprise, I don't think you're macho."

Millie gazed at him in disbelief. "I beat up a mugger once. I mean, he was *terrified*."

"The guy who tried to rob this place?"

"Before that. I was in Birmingham with that fellow who trampled my heart. We were walking to the car after a concert at the civic center, and a guy tried to hold us up. My date was ready to give in, but I—" She looked down at the hands she'd clasped tightly in her lap. "I said 'Hell, no,' and went on a rampage. The Birmingham police gave me a special commendation for civilian bravery."

Brig laughed until he saw the chagrined expression on her face. "Love, I'm not laughin' at you. It's just that I can imagine you poundin' the hell out of some unsuspectin' buzzard. I'm proud of you."

Her green eyes widened. "Why?"

"It's excitin'."

"But not sexy."

"*And* sexy."

"Bullfeathers," she muttered.

The expression on his weathered face became serious and thoughtful. "So this bloke who was with you didn't approve of you defendin' the both of you?"

"He was humiliated. It was the beginning of the end for us." Millie thumped one knee in frustration. "I had tried for so long to be what he wanted. And in one night, I ruined everything."

"You didn't ruin *anything*, love. You don't belong with a poofdah."

"A poofdah?"

Brig held up one hand, then let it dangle limply from the wrist.

Despite her intense feelings, Millie choked back a chortle. "He wasn't a poofdah."

"What was he, then?"

"He was one of the governor's top-ranking assistants. He wore expensive three-piece suits with monogrammed silk handkerchiefs in the breast pockets. He quoted Shakespeare, and when we went to French restaurants, he ordered in French. People always referred to him by his full name—John Franken Hepswood *the Fifth*. That ought to tell you something."

"And you tried to be the perfect uppercrust political girlfriend."

"I nearly made it too."

"You never would have lasted, love. There's too much fightin' blood in you."

Tears rose to her eyes. "I know."

"Melisande," he said huskily. "Don't cry."

"I'm not." A pair of tears slipped down her cheeks nonetheless, but not because of the past. She cried because suddenly she realized that her grand passion for John Franken Hepswood The Fifth paled in comparison to the emotions she felt looking at Brig, a near stranger. She wanted to come apart inside the arms of the man who was stretched out on her rooftop wearing only western boots and convict's pants, his chest glistening with sweat.

She wanted to fall in love with a man whose weathered face bespoke a lifetime of adventure, a man who liked her simply because she could provide more of the same. She wanted him like the sun wants to shine. And she knew that she could never have him.

"I'm not going to try to change to suit a man again," she murmured. "I know now that I'd eventually be miserable. It wouldn't work."

"I'm happy with you the way you are," he whispered.

Millie stared at him for a moment, then added slowly, "The way I look, you mean. I'm not talking about being pretty—"

"There are lots of pretty women in the world, Melisande. You're tip-top, but that's not what makes you special."

She didn't believe him, but she wanted so badly to believe him that she forgot common sense and, reaching out swiftly, stroked his cheek with the backs of her fingers. "You're a grand liar, mate," she rebuked softly, mimicking his accent.

"Aw . . ."

"I'm not special. I'm different. My father and brothers were afraid the whole world would take advantage of me because I was little and cute, so they taught me to be dangerous and unbreakable."

"I don't want to break you, love. Let me learn all about you, and then if you *do* break, I'll put you back together better than before."

Brig grasped her hand and kissed the palm. He kissed it a second time, his mouth firm and damp, while his eyes burned her with a serious, hungry look.

Millie looked away but found only more temptation as she watched the harsh rise and fall of his chest. She thought desperately that she didn't want this, this reckless impulse she fought to control every time she was near him. He made muscle and bone seem to soften inside her until she could concentrate on nothing but the need for his touch. Her breasts were swollen now, and her body was damp in ways that had nothing to do with external temperatures.

Millie knew he could see how hungry she was for everything he offered. She could argue and try to ignore it, but she craved the pleasure he gave so boldly. Would it be so terrible to take that simple pleasure and pretend that nothing else mattered?

Her voice came out raspy and low. "If we got involved, it would be so easy to pretend that we were perfect together."

He licked her palm with the tip of his tongue. "We *would* be perfect."

"If I weren't a deputy and you weren't a prisoner. If you didn't have to leave Paradise Springs when your sentence ends. If I thought I was right for you."

"Dammit, you *are* right for me."

"In some ways." She tilted her head and gave him a look of determination. "We're both fighters."

"It's not the fightin' I admire as much as the spirit," he corrected.

"And if the spirit proved to be too untraditional?"

"Melisande, I'm not like that fellow you left in Birmingham."

"You don't know me very well. And I don't know you."

His blue eyes glittered fiercely. "You know me. You know that you've met your match."

She nodded immediately. "And maybe I don't want to spend the rest of my life looking for someone to take your place after you're gone."

He pulled abruptly and forcefully on her hand, and she lost her balance on the angled roof, flinging out her free hand. He caught it, too, then drew her forward. She sprawled on his chest, and he held her hands behind his head so that she couldn't move away from him.

"Why the hell do you look on the dark side of everything?" he demanded. "You don't want a man to humiliate you again because you're not like other women. Fine. But that's a sloppy excuse for avoidin' me."

"I've read articles about you," she told him crisply. "You're *very* traditional. You told a reporter from the *Atlanta Journal* that most men want a woman who's soft and helpless."

He exhaled in exasperation. "But in the next breath I told the yahoo that I myself fancy women who can wrestle crocodiles and raise hell. That they make life more interestin'. The mangy devil didn't print *that* line though. Got me in trouble up to my eyeballs with all the women's libbers." His voice rose dramatically. "I don't want to defend my masculine pride anymore!" He let go of her hands and squinted his eyes shut. "Have at me! I'll just lay here and prove that I can be sensitive, like that bloke on the talk show."

"Who?" she asked breathlessly.

"Phil Donahue! Go on! Abuse me! I won't make a move to stop you!"

His outrageous teasing was too much. Partly to tease back, partly because she couldn't help herself, Millie put a hand on the side of his throat and stroked gingerly.

"Go on, go on! I can take it, Melisande! If you want me to prove that I don't mind aggressive women, I'll just lay still and show you!"

"You suffer *so* nobly."

Feeling like a kid tempted to steal candy but terrified

of the consequences, she propped herself on one elbow and let her hand trail slowly across his chest. His torso was the ultimate masculine promise—so much muscle, so much power, covered by ruddy skin and patterns of brown hair.

I shouldn't do this. He'll take advantage of the situation. I'll deserve the trouble, if he does. Stop, girl, stop! His arms lay above his head. She reached out and brushed her trembling fingertips along the corded paths of vein and sinew on one forearm. She had learned early in life to admire strength of purpose. How could she help but admire this man who wouldn't give up?

Millie flattened her hand over his heart and gauged its rapid beat. Her own heart was in sync. She ran her hand over his chest, molding her small fingers to the ridge of a rib, then watching rich brown hair curl over her nails as she slid her hand to the center of his stomach. A taut muscle fluttered underneath her touch, and Millie looked quickly at Brig's face.

Even though he still had his eyes closed, there was nothing peaceful about his expression. A mask of determination accentuated the laugh lines around his eyes and mouth. His lips were slightly parted, and when her hand slid lower on his stomach, he inhaled audibly.

She glanced down his body and whimpered at the visible sign of her effect straining against the soft white fabric of his pants. Power. That was what they shared, and Millie knew then that she could ruin him just as easily as he might ruin her. And he *would* ruin her, she knew very well. He lived his personal and professional life in a harsh spotlight. He needed a woman who could smooth his rough edges and keep him out of trouble, and she was just the opposite. Eventually he'd realize that fact.

Choking back a cry of frustration, Millie bent forward, kissed a spot over his heart, then rested her cheek against the center of his chest. His heartbeat was stronger now.

"Melisande, I'm crazy about you," he whispered.

But before his arms could surround her, she pushed herself away and stood up. He opened his eyes and studied her troubled expression, then grimaced as if he'd read her mind.

"I practically begged you to make me hot just now," he murmured. "Don't feel guilty."

"We can't, Brig," she told him wretchedly. "We just can't take this any further. Not ever."

She turned and made her way carefully across the roof to the ladder, then climbed down. Brig rose and walked to the gnarled carcass of the oak tree, then knelt by the torn place and looked down into her house. A minute later he heard water running in a sink somewhere below him. He could picture her splashing water on her face, trying to wash away her quiet torment. She had been taught not to think of herself as a woman, that women were a certain way and men another, that she didn't fit in.

Brig's eyes narrowed in concentration. When he got through with her, she'd know beyond a doubt that she was the best kind of woman and that she fit into his life perfectly.

Four

Early the next morning Suds dropped Brig off to work on her roof again. Millie was still drinking her morning tea as she went out to meet him. His skin and hair glowed from a recent scrubbing, and his white shirt was tucked neatly into spotless white trousers. He was a tonic that made her hands tremble, and Millie stared at him helplessly as he ambled up the pebbled walkway framed by multi-hued flower beds on either side. He stopped at the bottom step, then smiled at her, his blue eyes sleepy but devilish. His guitar case hung from one brawny hand.

"Good morning, Melisande," he said with the innocent tone of a schoolboy greeting a teacher. "Fine morning, eh?"

She shivered inwardly as she inhaled the warm scents of fresh soap and masculine skin. "Good morning, Brigand," she answered equally primly. Light-hearted banter would keep them both out of trouble, Millie hoped. "You don't see many mornings, I suspect."

He frowned mildly. "I'm a night person. Comes with my work."

"You could learn to love watching the sunrise."

Brig squinted at her, amused. "It's just a sunset in

reverse. But at sunset, at least my eyes are focused and I can think."

"I won't ask you to do anything mental until after nine."

"Make it ten," he corrected. His wide, generous mouth hinted at naughtiness. "I'll have to let my physical impulses run wild until then."

She wore another pair of cutoffs—loose ones, left a discreet length—and a floppy white T-shirt with a bright red road-race logo across the chest. He ducked his head a little, tilted it to one side, and gazed at her lithe, muscular legs. Again, his voice was innocent. "You've got goose bumps on your knees, love. Are you cold?"

Millie smiled at his tactics while she suppressed another small shiver. There would be no repeat of yesterday's rooftop scene. She pressed a hand to her chest, then told him, "Cold hearted. And don't forget it."

"Tsk, tsk." He shook his head. "Exercise would warm you up."

She wasn't going to ask what he had in mind. "I'll help you cut down the rest of the tree."

He sighed. "Wouldn't give a fellow a cup of hot coffee, would you?"

"I doubt *you* need warming up, but I'll be glad to provide a cup of blackberry tea. I don't have any coffee."

"How can a man work without stimulation? I'll have to look for something else to get my blood goin'."

She continued to smile, and silently admitted that she both loved and feared his provocative silliness. "I could turn the hose on you."

He gasped comically. "Ow."

Millie nodded toward the guitar case. "Heckuva lunch box." Brig laughed, the sound low and gruff. It echoed through her, loosening her knees and making her skin tingle. She took a quick swallow of tea and stepped back from his intense, disturbing presence.

"You can leave it inside." With a slight movement of her head she indicated the house behind her. "Come on. I'll fix your tea."

"Tea sounds fine, Melisande."

Brig's gaze followed her as she turned and went swiftly to the door, her bare feet padding delicately on the porch's creaking, whitewashed boards. Her feet were beautifully shaped and fine-boned. Slender blue veins crisscrossed the tops. He frowned as he felt blood pounding low in his body. It was going to be a long day, if he reacted this strongly to something as ordinary as feet. But then, nothing was ordinary about Melisande.

Her living room was a cluttered, likable place filled with family photographs, overstuffed furniture, and heavy, plain bookcases. Brig put his guitar case on a chintz-covered couch and trailed after her to the kitchen, where a bay window looked out on the majestic forest in the backyard.

She pointed to a small table in front of the window. "Have a seat."

"Yes, Melisande," he said quaintly, and folded his sturdy frame into a chair.

Millie could feel his eyes on her as she lifted a copper tea kettle from the white stove that was older than she was, then poured steaming water into a pottery mug. Her fingers trembling, she dunked a tea bag into the mug and brought it to the table. Her body felt like a tightly wound toy that was simply waiting for his touch to set it in motion. It was going to be a long day.

"Here," she said bluntly, and thumped the mug down.

"Easy, now, easy," he murmured. "Don't get skittish."

"Quit provoking me."

"I'm sorry, m'dear."

She put her hands on her hips. "The hell you are."

Still sitting down, he put his hands on *his* hips, then arched one brown brow at her. "You're right. I'm not sorry." Taken back by his honesty, she faltered for words.

"Shush," he ordered. "I'm not gonna lay a finger on you, but I'd be less than a man if I didn't enjoy the view."

She gestured toward her loose clothes. "I didn't mean to provide a view."

He turned toward the window, clasped his hands on

the table in an attitude of peaceful reverence, and stared out. In an absurdly royal voice he intoned, "The trees are just *ex-quis-it*."

Millie sputtered with a combination of frustration and traitorous laughter. "That's a terrible imitation of Prince Charles. Drink your tea, you Aussie hound. How about a biscuit with jelly and butter?"

He angled around a bit in the chair, his somewhat battered nose lifted high, his hands still clasped, his mouth drawn in fastidious concentration. "Thank you *ever* so kindly."

"Right," she muttered, smiling despite herself.

Afterwards they climbed to the roof and worked at reducing the huge oak tree to a limbless trunk. Insects sang in the woods around them, the sound as vibrant as summer, rising in operatic choruses and then falling to a mere whisper. The humidity made Millie's clothes cling to her body, and every time she glanced at Brig she was treated to the heart-stopping outline of his legs and hips under his own clinging clothes.

He bent over a massive limb, the chain saw roaring in his hands, wood chips flying. His forearms were corded with straining muscles. Sweat trailed down the center of his throat and disappeared under his white T-shirt. He'd discarded the outer shirt almost immediately. His expression was content. He was the kind of man who enjoyed using his body to the fullest. He raised his head for a moment and winked at her. She winked back, smiled tentatively, then looked away.

They worked together in silent harmony, surrounded and secluded in a sensual springtime world with no one but each other for company. Millie wondered if Jacques and Melisande had worked together like this, quietly, enjoying each other's presence, feeling the rich promise of the day and the hinted excitement of the night.

A knot twisted under her breastbone. She would share no nights with Brig here, no matter how much he tempted her. Jacques and Melisande knew they were together forever. Millie knew only that she'd never forget Brig when he left.

But when he stopped working and stripped the T-shirt from his torso, she had to force her eyes to remain on the saw clutched in her hand. She continued cutting a small limb, desperately focusing on the back and forth motion. Even when she heard him thump the chain saw down and walk toward her, she didn't look up.

"Melisande."

The low, rebuking way he said her name told her immediately that he recognized an avoidance technique when he saw one. She straightened and squinted up at him, trying to appear nonchalant.

"Yes?"

He had folded his T-shirt into a square. Slowly he cupped her chin in one hand, then smoothed the soft cotton over her face. "You're all perspire-ee. Take a break and let me wipe you down," he murmured. Hypnotized, she simply stood still. He moved the T-shirt over her face, dabbing at her cheeks, drawing swathes of sensation across her mouth.

"You're pink," he whispered. "You look sexy as hell."

When he stroked the material down her throat, she closed her eyes and tilted her head back. Brig's thumb caressed the pulse point under her chin. His voice came to her dimly, through the roaring in her ears. "You're too hot, love," he whispered. "I wouldn't want you to faint."

She opened her eyes and looked at him, feeling groggy. Her pulse had been fine until a moment ago. Now it raced so hard that she could barely think. Millie reached out and placed her fingertips under his chin. His skin was slick and burning, the blood pounding beneath her touch. "Seems to me," she said huskily, "that we're both too hot."

"There are ways to take care of that."

She nodded, picturing the way he had in mind, seeing them both naked on the pink satin sheets of her bed. "Iced tea," she said vaguely. She drew her hand away from his throat. His fingers were still curved against her neck, their effect so powerful that he seemed to be touching her all over.

One corner of his mouth lifted in a rueful smile. "Iced tea'll have to do for now."

He let his hand trail along her neck to the collar of her shirt. Millie waited breathlessly, only half-wanting to protest, as his fingertips continued downward. He touched the curve of her breast, feathered his hand over it, then brushed his thumb across the imprint that couldn't be hidden by her bra or shirt. Millie nearly groaned as her nipple tightened instantly, betraying the loss of her last shred of willpower. The breath cascaded out of her lungs in a low, shuddering, "*Stop.*"

His eyes challenged her while his thumb circled and tantalized. "If you really don't like it, all you have to do is move away," he instructed hoarsely.

Millie made a strangled, angry sound at his confident intuition. She'd show him. She pushed his hand away and took two large steps straight back—right onto the thin sheet of plastic covering the hole in her roof. They both realized her mistake. The plastic ripped like a piece of paper.

"Melly, grab my hand!" Brig yelled.

He lunged for her, but only succeeded in grabbing a wisp of her hair as she plummeted through the roof. Brig's blood turned to ice water as he watched her hit the corner of her bed and slide to the floor in a limp heap.

He grasped the sides of the hole, slipped both feet into it, and lowered himself into her bedroom. He let go and dropped feetfirst onto her bed. With a cracking sound, the slats under the mattress and box spring gave way, dumping a corner onto the floor. Caught off balance, Brig landed on his rump and slid down beside Millie.

She lifted her head weakly and looked at him. "You make a heckuva entrance," she managed to say before she closed her eyes and moaned. "SuperAussie to the rescue."

He grasped her head between his hands and scrutinized her white face. "Where does it hurt?"

"Here." She raised a hand and touched the side of her head.

"You musta hit a rafter, love."

"No, it's where you pulled my hair out."

He drew one hand back and they both looked at the strands of blond hair caught between his fingers. "Caveman," she teased, her eyes squinted nearly shut. Millie shifted slightly, then winced. Immediately he slipped an arm around her and turned her so that she could lean against his chest. Millie let her head drape back on his bare shoulder.

"What is it?" he asked tensely. "What hurts, you tough Sheila? Speak up."

"I'm little, that's all. I got the breath knocked out of me, and I don't have that much breath to lose. Just give me a minute to recuperate." Brig stroked her hair and kissed her forehead as she inhaled shakily. "Are *you* all right?" she asked.

"Sure. Landed on my butt. That's the toughest part of me."

She chuckled. "You should have landed on your hard head."

His voice was taut with self-rebuke. "It was my fault that you fell through the roof."

"Sssh. You didn't exactly push me, Brig. Forget it."

He sighed. "You sure do bounce good."

"An admiral told me the same thing once. I fell out of a tree trying to retrieve his wife's pet ferret."

Brig propped her against the side of the bed and crouched by her legs, straightening them out slowly. "Does anything hurt yet?"

"Nope."

"Move your toes." He cupped the toes of her bare foot in his hand. She wrapped her big toe and second toe around his forefinger and gripped hard. "Strewth! Let go, you monkey!"

Smiling, she pulled her foot away. "My brothers taught me to pinch with my toes."

"Remind me to thank the blokes," he told her wryly. Brig bent his head and placed a smacking kiss on her toes.

Millie eyed him askance. "My feet are sandy."

He shrugged. "A little sand never hurt anybody." Then he dropped her foot, made a great show of wiping his mouth, and groaned, "Where's the john? I think I have to throw up."

She laughed a little and shoved him with her foot.

"Want to wrestle, do you?" he asked, relief written in his expression. "If you hadn't just walloped the floor, I'd show you a thing or two."

"Excuses, excuses," she challenged, grinning. Millie leaned forward and shook her fist at him. "I grew up wrestling with two mean brothers, and . . ." Her teasing bravado faded and she sat back gingerly.

"Melisande?" Brig got on his knees and grasped her shoulders. Her green eyes were dark with discomfort.

"Must have pulled a muscle in my back."

"Damned fightin' woman," he grumbled anxiously. "Don't know when to sit still."

"Be quiet, hound."

He got up, rigged the boxspring and mattress back into place using the slats that hadn't broken, then squatted beside her and put his hands under her arms. "Up you go, love. Squawk if it hurts."

"I definitely will."

But he was so careful and so strong that he raised her to a sitting position on the bed's edge without jarring her back at all. He knelt in front of her, his hands sliding down to her waist. Millie raised her arms tentatively and stretched.

"It's just a twinge," she said truthfully. "It'll loosen up in a minute, and we can go back to the roof."

"I have my doubts. Lay on your stomach and let old Doc McKay's magic fingers do some massagin'."

Millie studied him shrewdly. He apparently had no intentions other than to rub her aching back. "Okay."

His hands were deliciously strong on her sides as he

helped her turn and arrange herself face down on the rumpled bed. She felt very vulnerable.

Brig sat down beside her and stifled the thick, inarticulate sound of pleasure that rose in his throat. She looked so tempting with her blond hair tossled on a white pillow etched in pink eyelet and her head turned to one side so that he could see her flushed face. He wondered if her complexion would look that way after sex, then reminded himself sternly that she was hurt.

"Excuse me, love," he said, and with no more than that warning he pulled the back of her T-shirt up to her neck. "Excuse me, love," he said again, and deftly unhooked her bra.

Millie gasped lightly. "Your apologies are suspicious."

His accent deepened. "Ah, but me heart's good."

He flattened his hands beneath her shoulder blades and stroked down to the top of her blue-jean shorts, enjoying the smoothness of her skin. With one forefinger he traced a tiny dark mole in the small of her back. "Beauty mark," he noted softly. "Beautiful back." Brig pressed his fingers into the area just above her shorts and rubbed small circles.

Millie shifted languidly, wishing that he didn't make it so easy to forget caution. His touch untied her muscles and drew sensations from low in her body.

"Do you know what's best for this kind of muscle strain?" he asked.

"Ice pack," she murmured, and found that her lips had trouble forming words. What was the man doing? Mesmerizing her?

"Nope. Moist heat." He bent over and placed his damp, hot lips into the curve of her back.

Millie shut her eyes tightly and willed herself to protest. The words were almost spoken when he slid his mouth up her spine, dabbing each vertebra with the tip of his tongue. Speech, she realized quickly, was an impossibility. Nothing had ever felt so good.

Brig stopped at the base of her neck and nibbled gently. Then he reversed the journey, tracing her spine back down to the edge of her shorts. When he circled her beauty mark with his tongue, she simply moaned and gave up.

"You can stop doing that in about a million years," Millie whispered.

"No harm in it, eh?"

"Plenty of harm. But I'm only human."

"Female human. Without a doubt." He began kissing her shoulder blades, his breath brushing her skin in warm puffs. The fingers of one hand trailed up and down her spine. "A woman with all sorts of womanly feelings." His fingers curled around her waist and stroked upwards to the sides of her breasts. She shivered as he rubbed lightly. "Melisande," he whispered in a husky tone, "this part of you is so soft and delicate." He chuckled, the sound strained. "I've got just the right hard parts to go with your soft ones."

Millie tried to take a breath, only to hear a shallow, ragged sound. "Stop. Oh, *please*, stop." She raised her head and pushed clenched fists into the bed.

He pressed her down again. "Sssh. Relax. We'll talk about safer things, love."

She sighed heavily. "Nothing is safe with you."

His hands moved with wicked skill over her back, coaxing her to relax again. "I can behave," he assured her. "Now, let's see . . . the navy. Tell me why you left the navy."

Millie hugged the pillow under her head and tried to arrange her whirling thoughts. After a moment, she said quietly, "The military still isn't a good place for a woman. No matter how competent you are, you're still a woman doing a man's job. Everyone treats you like some sort of experimental toy. Sexual harassment is a way of life."

"But you're not a quitter. What made you give it up?" She frowned and was silent. He grasped her shoulders and squeezed. "Talk, Melisande. I keep secrets like a miser keeps money. You're safe with me."

Tears came to her eyes. She *did* feel safe with him, even though he kept up a running assault on her resistance. "I was assigned to the shore patrol at one of the Pacific bases. There weren't many women there, and I was the only one who wasn't a secretary or a nurse. The commanding officer decided I was eccentric, and he made my life miserable. He cornered me one night and said he was going to teach me how a normal woman enjoys a man."

Brig's voice was rough. "I reckon you showed him that a normal woman can fight like hell."

She smiled against the pillow. "He didn't walk without limping for two days." The smile faded. "I filed a complaint, and there was a hush-hush investigation. He got away with a slap on the wrist and I ended up looking like a troublemaker."

"Damn, Melly. Damn." He kissed the back of her neck in sympathy and rested his coarse masculine cheek there. They were both silent for a moment.

"Brig? No one but you knows that story. I didn't want my brothers to find out that I was attacked. Kyle and Jeopard work in navy intelligence—very important stuff, and they have solid careers. They think I left the navy because I got tired of sexism, which is basically true."

"But why—"

"They'd have located that officer and beaten the hell out of him," she explained grimly. "They still might, if they found out. I won't let them risk their careers that way."

"I like your brothers, and I haven't even met them."

"If you think I'm a tough cookie, you should meet Kyle and Jeopard."

Brig stroked a hand over her hair, letting his fingertips brush her forehead. "Sounds like a good family to be part of. I've never had a close family. Never missed it, until lately."

"Lately?" she murmured.

He chuckled. "I get pictures in my mind of babies with blond hair and Aussie accents."

Her eyes flew open and she started to speak, but he pressed a restraining finger against her lips. That intimate contact was enough to make her close her eyes again. Brig traced her lips with his fingertip.

"There's a good girl," he whispered. "She knows when to just listen."

"Poof," she said against his finger, blowing an exasperated breath.

He laughed hoarsely. "*Poof* yourself, love. I'm a patient man."

"Who talks a nice tale."

He patted her rump. "Nice tail."

"Stop it, convict." Trembling, she raised her head, squinted at him in sincere warning, and brushed away the conniving finger that was now drawing invisible lines along her jawline. "I mean it, Brig. I'm still a deputy."

"I know. I'm just givin' aid to an injured law officer."

"My fanny isn't injured."

He sighed. "Too bad."

The resigned look he gave her was so calculated and so ridiculous that she buried her head in the pillow to hide her smile.

"I know what you're doin' ," he said coyly. "Because you got a dimple beside your mouth, and it only shows up when you smile. I can see that dimple."

"Bullfeathers," she said, her voice muffled. He ran his hands down her bare sides, tickling. "Brig!" She twisted away and sat up, then stared down at herself. Her T-shirt and bra were bunched under her arms. Brig's gaze went unabashedly to her full breasts. Amusement shown in his blue eyes, but under the amusement were more primitive emotions.

Millie calmly crossed her arms over her chest. "My bosom isn't injured, *either*," she assured him. She tingled all over, as if he'd pulled her apart carefully and left her that way, aching for the time when he would put her back together.

He took a deep breath and smiled nonchalantly. Now was the time, he thought, to let well enough alone. He'd accomplished a lot in the last few minutes. Restraint was hell, though, because he'd never wanted anything so much in his life as to wrap his arms around her voluptuous little body and kiss her exasperated mouth.

"Melisande, if you tense up, your back'll hurt."

"My back is *fine*." She winced a little as she said it.

"Lay down and cover your rosy nekidness before I strain my eyes from tryin' to peek. I'll get my guitar and play you some songs."

"The roof—"

"Can wait a while."

He left the room, whistling. Millie rearranged her bra and T-shirt, then lay back on the bed. Her back *was* aching, and a deliciously cool breeze was drifting in from the large window nearby. She watched the white curtains flutter and listened intently to the distant sounds of Brig moving about her cottage. What would Jacques and Melisande think of this rugged, take-charge man? Millie knew instinctively that they'd feel a kinship with him.

He came back carrying his guitar and a tall glass full of beer. He laid the guitar on the bed near her feet, inhaled the breeze, and rubbed his bare chest briskly. Millie watched him through slitted eyes, trying not to look as affected as she felt. He had no belt for his white work trousers, and they hung below his navel. It was a wonderful navel . . . she shut her eyes.

"Feels great in here," he said heartily. "Place doesn't even need an air conditioner." He held the beer aloft and toasted solemnly. "Great-great-great-granddaddy and grandma, you did a helluva job."

He downed half the beer in one swallow, then sat on the bed and handed her the glass. He propped pillows behind her and then picked up his guitar. Millie sipped beer and watched his large, work-roughened hands cradle the instrument lovingly.

"Now, Miss Melisande," he said in a low, soothing voice, "Just you take it easy. Any requests?"

She bit her tongue to keep from saying in a moment of utter recklessness, *Yes, but you'll have to put the guitar down.* "Nope."

He nodded, and began to play.

Rucker McClure took one hand off the steering wheel, let it creep slyly across the rental car's plush seat, and curled his fingers into the skirt of his wife's yellow sundress. She had her head bowed over a thick hardback titled *Political Reform in South America*, and her long, chocolate-colored hair hung forward in gentle waves, hiding a face with classical features.

Rucker inched the material of her skirt up until he could see most of one golden thigh. He smiled, pleased with his subterfuge. His fingers hovered nearer their conquest, ready to sample the beautiful leg.

"Sir, I *know* what you're up to," she said in a husky, educated voice, without looking up from her book. "And if you don't behave, I'll throw you in the backseat and take advantage of you."

"Oh, *yes*, ma'am," he drawled in the deep accent of the rural South. Then he slipped his fingers over her thigh and lazily caressed the smooth, warm skin.

"You asked for it." She snapped the book shut, tossed it to the floor, and twisted quickly toward him. One hand roamed devilishly over the front of his faded jeans while the other grabbed his jaw. Tilting his head toward her, she nuzzled his dark mustache and gave him a smacking kiss on the mouth, then burrowed her face against his neck.

"Dee, don't you dare leave any marks!" he protested comically, as she growled and placed gentle bites along his throat. "Millie'll be shocked!"

She laughed softly. "She told me a long time ago that *nothing* you can do shocks her." Dinah Sheridan McClure, known to her husband as *Dee* and sometimes, when Rucker wanted to provoke her, as *DeeDee*, paused between kisses long enough to add, "This is a vacation. I'm entitled to be wild."

Rucker turned the car off the main road down a sandy driveway that wound into a hardwood forest. "Not right this minute! Straighten yourself up, woman!"

he ordered, grinning and shoving her hand away from the zipper on his jeans.

"You always ask for trouble. Now you've got it."

"I'll walk funny when I get out of the car! Whoa!"

Chuckling, she moved back to her own side and sat quietly, smiling at him as they pulled up to Millie's cottage. They stared at the remnants of the giant tree that still sagged against one corner of the structure, and their teasing mood faded.

Both feeling a little anxious, they hurried to the porch. The wooden door stood open, and when Rucker tested the screen door, it was unfastened. There were no sounds but the rustling of breezes in the forest and the chatter of birds.

Rucker and Dinah shared a worried look. He knocked loudly. "Millie?" No answer. His mouth grim, Rucker pulled the door open.

They stepped into the silent cottage and glanced around the living room. Pacing his steps carefully, Rucker moved down a short hallway to the bedroom, Dinah tiptoeing right behind him. He halted at the bedroom door and she peered over his shoulder. They stared for several long seconds.

"Well, I'll be damned," Rucker said loudly, and began to grin.

Dinah slapped his shoulder. "Rucker, sssh."

"Wake up, Miss Hunstomper!"

Miss Hunstomper. Millie hadn't heard that affectionate term since she stopped working for Rucker McClure. It was the name by which he'd referred to her in his columns. Now it made her eyes fly open.

She was on her back, and the first thing she saw was Brig's head, his hair mussed. *All* she saw was hair, because he had his face practically buried between the mattress and her left breast. She could feel his slow, even breathing even through her T-shirt. He lay on his side with his legs drawn up below her hips. He was curled around her. Millie's legs were propped on top of him, the back of her knees draped over the top of his thigh. His arm lay across her stomach.

Still disoriented from deep sleep, she jerked her head toward the bedroom door and squinted her eyes. Only one deep, familiar voice could do justice to *Miss Hunstomper*, and it belonged to the tall, mustached man in running shoes, jeans, and a sport shirt.

Rucker. Dinah. Reality flooded back. Humiliation followed. "Brig!" She sat up and shook Brig's shoulder harshly. "Wake up!"

He yawned, didn't open his eyes, and tightened his arm across her stomach. "Aw, Melisande, go back to sleep. I'm harmless." He yawned again. "You went to sleep . . . and I got sleepy watchin' you. Love, you're fantastic to cuddle. Like a little koala bear." He went back to sleep.

Millie's face burned. She glanced at Rucker and Dinah. Dinah had her husband by the arm, trying to tug him away from the door.

"I'm sorry, Millie," she said, looking chagrined. "We should have called first. We just flew into Gainesville this morning, and we're on our way to visit Rucker's mother. We stopped by the jail to see you, but the sheriff said you were off today."

Millie sighed. "Don't go. Wait a minute." She bent over and spoke loudly in Brig's ear. "I have company!"

He stirred finally, shoved himself up to one elbow, ran a hand through his hair, then tried to focus on Rucker and Dinah. "G'day, folks," he murmured.

"Good lord," Rucker said softly. "I know you."

"Give me a second, and maybe *I'll* remember who I am."

"He's Brig McKay," Millie said quickly, and pushed herself away from him. She swung her legs off his thigh and rose from the bed. "He's serving a jail term, but today he's supposed to be working on my roof. Brig, this is my old boss, the writer, Rucker McClure, and his wife, Dinah."

"Yeah! Hello, mate! Did you like the beer?"

"Loved it. What's the story here? Looks like a great one. What are you doin' in jail?"

Millie glared at Rucker. Her life was truly falling apart.

"You're not going to write about this. I'd like to keep my embarrassment private."

"He won't write about it," Dinah assured her.

"But I'm sure nosy enough to want some explanation," Rucker added.

Millie nodded, defeated. "Let's go in the kitchen and fix some tea."

"Tea settles her nerves," Brig added solemnly.

Rucker and Dinah left two hours later, considerably better informed than upon their arrival. Before their departure, Dinah drew Millie into the privacy of the bedroom, grasped her shoulders, and looked down at her knowingly.

"There's a lot going on between you and Brig McKay."

Millie hesitated a moment, then gave up. "I guess that little scene in the bedroom confirms it."

Dinah shook her head. "Not just that. It's the way he watches you. You said once that you hoped some man would look at you the way Rucker looks at me. Well, you've found that man."

That idea sent a disturbing wave of hope through Millie. At the same time, she couldn't forget the odds against having a permanent relationship with Brig. She shook her head. "He needs a Barbie Doll. I'm a G.I. Josephine."

The smile that flitted across Dinah's mouth disappeared as soon as she saw that Millie was serious. "I'd say that you're not giving him a chance."

"You're wrong." Millie hugged her. "I'm on the verge of throwing in the towel and following him like a lost puppy. Do you know what I mean?" She stepped back, watching Dinah nod and smile gently.

"Even when I was most terrified of letting Rucker into my life, I couldn't stop wanting him."

"It's frightening. And I'm not used to being afraid of anything or anyone."

Dinah patted her shoulder. "It's good to be afraid of

someone who has the power to hurt you. But just remember—he has the power to make you happy too."

Millie was still mulling over those words as she watched Rucker and Dinah leave. When their car disappeared around a bend in the driveway, she turned toward Brig, who stood beside her. Thankfully, he'd put his shirt back on soon after Rucker and Dinah's arrival. At least she wouldn't have to concentrate so hard on keeping her gaze above his neck.

"Back to the roof," she said firmly. "No more nap time."

The tiniest of smiles played on his mouth, but he said nothing. When they were back on the roof, he sat down to oil the chain saw blade. As he worked, he commented casually, "Rucker and Dinah have got something special."

Millie, who had just knelt by a limb she intended to cut, looked up with a thoughtful expression. "I've never known two people who loved each other more."

"But they're not exactly a perfect pair, you know. Her bein' the mayor of that place in Alabama. What's the name of it?"

"Mount Pleasant."

"Yeah, and bein' so scholarly and an ex-beauty queen. She's the kind of woman you'd picture marryin' an ambassador or a professor or somethin'. Instead, she's married to a hell-raisin' old farm boy who made good. And it works just fine." He cocked one brow at her. "Isn't that interestin'? A mismatched couple sort of like you and me, eh?"

"Oh? Are you an ex-beauty queen?"

"Melisande, you she-devil, you know what I mean."

Millie cleared her throat and gave him an indulgent look. "I'll tell you something about Dinah. She served a year in prison for trying to protect her father, who was accused of embezzling. Rucker helped her clear her name. *That's* the kind of trust and sharing that makes two incompatible people realize they belong together."

Her attitude seeped down inside him and twisted his patience. So she didn't think she could have that kind of relationship with a man like him. Anger clouded Brig's voice. "And you don't want to trust anybody, 'cause you're so strong you don't *need* anybody, right?"

Millie realized that she'd wounded him. But he had just wounded her, in return. "Right."

"Helluva sad way to live a life. You might as well be a rock, for all the happiness you'll get."

She stood, her fists clenched. "I had a lot more happiness before *you* came along."

He uttered several choice and colorful words. "Yeah. Lady deputy—unemotional, unbreakable, untouchable. Nobody *wanted* to touch you. It was too much damned trouble to get through that hide of yours. What are you gonna be ten years from now?"

"Independent!"

He leaped to his feet and pointed at her. "I've got it! You'll stay here, you'll get promoted to sheriff, you'll get tougher and lonelier and sadder. Old spinster sheriff, lives all by herself in the middle of the woods, sorta peculiar, but she does a damned fine job—that's what folks'll say about you!"

"I don't want to hear your thumbnail analysis of my future!"

"You'll get some cats to keep you company, and everyone'll notice how you talk to the cats as if they were children. You'll get kinda picky and fussy and set in your ways. You'll go to bed early 'cause there's nothing else to do."

"*Be quiet!*" she shouted.

"Your brothers'll get married and have kids, and when you go to visit, the kids'll be scared of you! Your brothers will feel sorry for their poor sis. There used to be something fresh and loving about her, but now she's dried up!"

Millie shook with fury and anguish. He'd expertly probed her worst nightmare. "I'm leaving," she said in a tormented whisper, and threw down the saw. "I'll send Suds to pick you up at the end of the day."

Brig tossed his hands into the air and yelled, "Good! Run from me! Run from the truth!"

She fought for composure, but she could barely talk. Suddenly tears slipped down her face. "I don't run from the truth," she said brokenly. "I carry it with me everywhere I go. But . . . you really know how to make it *hurt*."

Millie wiped roughly at her eyes as she went to the ladder and climbed down. Stunned, Brig felt his anger drain away. He'd expected some fierce retort, not a wistful admission he was right. He'd just neatly ripped her apart, without even realizing it.

Seconds later, he heard her start the old convertible. She drove away from the cottage fast, without looking back.

Brig sank to his boot heels and ran a hand through his hair. His shoulders slumped. "Little Melisande, what have I done to you, love?" he whispered.

Five

She would not ache inside any longer, she would not think about the bleak future Brig painted for her, and she *would* shut him out of her emotions. The morning following his tirade Millie felt the ugly residue of his words as if he'd stained her for life.

She sat at the front desk, her hands shaking and stomach tight as she tried to concentrate on Charlie's report from the night shift. A Beatles medley was playing on the civilian radio under the desk; the song at the moment, "*Yesterday.*"

"How appropriate," she murmured under her breath, frowning.

She heard the door from the cell block swing open, but refused to look up, hoping the footsteps coming toward her belonged to Suds.

"G'morning," Brig said softly.

Humiliation combined with bittersweet determination to give her rigid control over her reactions. She raised her head slowly, her expression neutral except for one politely raised brow. He was leaning on the counter over her desk, a coffee mug in one big hand.

"Good morning. Do you need something?"

He looked troubled and tired. "Roof okay with you? The patching, I mean."

"Fine. You do good work."

"For a permanent fix you'll have to have a carpenter and roofer come on."

"I've already contacted someone."

"I could do the work, if you want. Probably take two, three days. When I was about half-grown, I worked on a construction crew."

She forced her voice to remain unemotional. "No, but thank you."

He made a small sound of disgust, rubbed a hand over his weathered face, and squinted at her shrewdly. "I'd be cheaper than a contractor."

"I don't want you to do the work." An edge of anger had crept into her tone, and she had emphasized each word.

"It's foolish to let personal feelings stand in the way of money matters."

"How ironic, considering that you're well-known for giving charity concerts. I like being foolish. Indulge me."

He slapped the counter top, all calm gone. "I'm *tryin'* to indulge you, you little Tasmanian devil!"

"Then leave me alone. That's all I ask."

His expression fierce, he jabbed a finger at her. "You're gonna make me bleed for the things I said yesterday, aren't you?"

Millie blinked hard, surprised. Then she realized he was right. She wanted to make him apologize. She wanted to hear him say that none of his words had been sincere. But deep down inside, she would always know he'd told her the truth.

She shook her head, and the energy drained out of her. Millie propped her elbows on the desk, cupped her chin in her hands, and looked up at him sadly. "You only confirmed what I already believe," she told him. "I'm glad you did it. I have to learn to live with the future."

Frowning, he stared at her for a moment. Then fury lit his eyes. "Dammit!" He turned and hurled the coffee mug against the nearest wall. The mug cracked into several large pieces and black liquid trailed down the wall's pristine gray wallpaper.

Millie stared at him wide-eyed as he whipped back toward her, fists clenched. He shook them in the air. "You wouldn't have to plan on a lonely future if you'd just let your guard down!" he shouted. "You don't know diddle about what makes a man think a woman's sexy!" He took several deep breaths, opened his hands in a gesture of surrender, and shook his head. "I've had it. I've tried my best, and it's a waste of time." He gave her an icy look. "I'll not bother you anymore, Melisande . . . excuse me, I mean *Millie*."

With that, he turned and strode back into the cell block, slamming the door behind him. Feeling numb, Millie went to the shattered coffee mug. She knelt beside it and began picking up the pieces. Raybo's office door slammed open and he stuck his head out, his phone glued perpetually to one hand.

"What kind of possum fight is goin' on out here?"

She considered for a moment. The hollowness inside her could have filled the Grand Canyon. "Nothing. I made a mess." He grunted and shut his door again. "Of everything," she whispered hoarsely.

Brig was good to his word, leaving her alone, being nothing more than coolly polite to her for the next week. He continued to call her *Millie*, which upset her more each time he said it. One afternoon she was standing by the office-supply closet, taking inventory, when he strolled past with a stack of paperbacks in one hand.

"Whatd'ya think of Stephen King?" he tossed over his shoulder.

"Like him."

"Me too. Been meanin' to read his latest, but couldn't get hold of a copy before I left Nashville."

Her heart pounding with the prospect of doing something nice for him, she said quickly, "I'll find it for you at the bookstore."

He went into his cell without a backward glance and shut the door. "Not to worry, Millie," he called. "I'll have one of my friends send me a copy."

She wasn't a friend, then. She was just Millie, someone he didn't want to care about anymore. She'd been chased by many men, but it had always seemed more like a burden than a compliment. She'd been grateful when they gave up.

This time she wanted to chase back. Disgusted with her mental meanderings, Millie wearily rested her head against the door to the supply closet and tried to absorb the inventory by osmosis.

She had night duty that Friday, and she arrived for work just as Brig finished a Chinese dinner. He and Suds were eating together in the deputy's lounge, their feet propped on a square, Formica-topped table, cartons and cups spread around them in nonchalant disarray. A small television on the wall was tuned to female wrestling matches.

"Look at this silliness, Millie," Brig instructed, pointing to the TV. He reached one long arm over and jerked a chair out for her. She sat down between him and Suds, eyeing Brig warily because she didn't know what to expect.

Millie glanced at the television and saw a pair of athletic-looking women clad in leotards circling each other in a ring. "So? They're making a living. I admire them."

Suds sighed. "They've got everything a man could want."

"Big muscles and lots of body hair," Brig added.

Millie sniffed. "*Very* cute, wise guy."

Suds chortled under his breath as he dumped his trash in a garbage can and headed for the door. "I'm gone for the night, Mel. Have a good one, Brig."

" 'Night, mate."

Silence descended on the jail. Millie kept her eyes glued to the television while a tiny rivulet of perspiration ran between her breasts.

Brig leaned back even further in his chair and put

both hands behind his head. "So it's just you and me, love," he said cheerfully. "All night."

"I have paperwork to do."

"Watch the wrestling with me awhile."

Millie smiled grimly. "You think it suits my aggressive tendencies?"

"Well, yeah, but the main thing is that it shows how sexy a fightin' woman can be. Look there." He pointed to the screen. "I was only teasin' about the muscles and hair. That tall girl is pure-blooded Cherokee Indian, and beautiful. Got a kick like a mule. And the men are goin' wild over her."

Millie listened to the studio crowd roar as a lithe, bronze-skinned young woman with long black hair gracefully kicked her opponent in the ribs. "I couldn't do that," Millie commented.

"Squeamish?"

"Legs are too short."

He grinned slowly, and then he laughed. The rich, vibrant sound reminded her of all she'd lost with him; of all she'd never have. Millie rose quickly, feeling miserable and trying to hide it. "I'll be up front, taking care of business."

Brig rocked on the back legs of his chair, assessing her through slitted eyes. His voice was droll. "I can sleep easy, then, knowin' that you're lookin' after me."

She smiled thinly and left the room. What would he do if she went wild and ravished him? Would it be the end of her career as a deputy, or the beginning or her career as a wrestler?

Weekends were relatively tame in Paradise Springs, and it wasn't unusual for a deputy to spend the night tossing paper airplanes at a geranium hanging across from the registration desk. Millie was surprised when the phone rang at two A.M.

She took the caller's frantic message, then ran back to the cell block. The light was on in Brig's cubicle, and she heard him playing the guitar. Millie slid to a stop by the door. He was stretched out on his bunk, the guitar resting on his stomach.

"I have to break up a domestic fight," she told him. "Just wanted you to know."

He got up quickly. "Let me go with you."

"No, no, no."

"I'll stay in the car. Dammit, Melisande, it's not safe for *anyone* to take on something like that without backup."

So he still thought of her as *Melisande*. Millie was so stunned and so pleased that she stared at him speechlessly. Resistance melted inside her. "Only if you *promise* to stay in the car."

He crossed his heart solemnly. "Swear on a kangaroo's hop."

"Is that considered binding by anything other than a kangaroo?"

Brig shrugged. "It's the best I can do."

She felt reckless. "All right, let's go."

The night wind gusted with the promise of thunderstorms. Lightning drew yellow streaks as crooked as a witch's fingers clawing the sky. The Hideaway Trailer Park on the outskirts of Paradise Springs was a quiet, middle-class place ordinarily, but tonight it seemed sinister. Alarmed neighbors stood outside a sleek blue double-wide trailer, their clothes and hair whipping in the wind. After Millie cut the patrol car's engine, she unlatched the restraining strap on her gun holster.

Brig was a large, soothing, and deceptively relaxed presence in the seat beside her. When she opened the car door, he didn't offer any patronizing cautions, but instead said gruffly, "Hurry back."

"Faster than a kangaroo's hop," she replied. Millie caught the white gleam of his smile before she left the car.

He watched her go up the steps to the trailer door, her curly blond hair buffeted, her small body swaying when the wind hit it. She knocked on the door and a stocky, disheveled woman threw it open. Millie stepped inside and shut the door behind her.

Brig cursed softly and dug his fingers into the car seat in order to keep himself from following her. In his culture men protected women, and this situation strained his tolerance to the breaking point. Besides, this wasn't just any woman, this was Melisande, the most aggravating, stubborn, mixed-up woman he'd ever met. She didn't know how to ask for help when she needed it—and that scared him.

He waited five minutes, then ten, his concern growing Fifteen minutes after she entered the trailer he heard a muffled scream. Brig was already out of the car when the trailer door opened. The interior lights silhouetted the stout husband of the brawling pair. He held a rolling pin in one hand. The milling neighbors hurriedly moved back from the threat.

Brig raced out of the darkness, leaped to the top doorstep, and broadsided the husband. Screams rose from the crowd. The man fell backward into the trailer's living room, with Brig on top of him. Brig glanced around, saw no one else, and grabbed the front of the sweaty sport shirt his victim wore.

"Where's the deputy, you bastard?"

The man was breathless from the fall. "Bathroom."

Brig jerked the rolling pin from his hand and threw it under a couch. He vaulted to his feet and ran toward a hallway.

Millie lay on her back on the floor, her head propped against the open bathroom door. She held a hand to one eye. The wife crouched beside her, crying.

"Melisande!" Brig went down on his knees and grasped her head between his hands.

"I got hit in the eye," she murmured with a hint of embarrassment. "It's not that bad."

He pulled her hand back and grimly studied the swelling purple bruise around her left eye. "I'll kill him," Brig muttered, and started to get up. Millie grabbed his shirt sleeve.

"No!"

'They can put me in jail for two more months, I don't care! What kind of man hits a woman *and* a law officer?"

"It was m-me," the woman interjected. She sobbed and raised a meaty fist. "I did it."

Stunned, Brig stared at her. "*Strewth*," he said. Then his expression darkened. "What the hell were you doin', whackin' a deputy that way?"

"You're a c-convict!" the woman said fearfully, noticing his outfit for the first time.

"It was an accident," Millie interjected. She sat up, and Brig helped her stand. She cleared her throat in a warning way that told him her duty was more important than an injury, so he removed his arm from her shoulders. As her eye swelled shut, she explained about the battle.

"Mrs. Brown had Mr. Brown trapped in the bathroom. I finally convinced her to let Mr. Brown come out, but when he did, there was a little scuffle and I was caught in the middle."

"What's this *convict* doing on the loose?" Mrs. Brown insisted, her voice rising. She backed away from Brig, clutching her hands to an ample bosom.

His eyes narrowed lethally and he made a growling sound. "Don't make me chase you, me little peach. The prison doctor says I shouldn't be *provoked*."

Millie sighed and hurriedly told her, "He isn't dangerous. I'm transporting him to a work detail."

"In the middle of the night?" Mrs. Brown asked.

Millie faltered for a second and Brig took up the slack. "I do my best work in the dark." His voice was wicked. Mrs. Brown took another step back.

"That'll be enough," Millie interjected quickly. She gave Brig a stern look. "Go back to the patrol car. On the double."

Brig bit his tongue and nodded. She was in charge here, and the grim set of her mouth told him that his continued assistance would make her look bad. Besides, she had the situation under control. Brig realized how proud he was of her. It was hell for him to turn on his boot heels and leave her alone with the Browns, but he did it. Melisande's dignity was all that mattered. And at that moment Brig knew how much he loved her.

Ten minutes later she came out of the trailer and told the crowd to go home, everything was fine. Her shoulders back and her chin up, she presented a picture of absolute command as she walked to the patrol car. Brig ached to reach for her when she slid into the driver's seat, but people would see. She shut the door and locked her seat belt in place with quick, assured hands.

"How's the shiner, love?"

Millie started the car and kept her eyes forward. "No sweat, mate."

She drove down a dark, windswept two-lane road. When they were out of sight from the trailer park, she pulled onto a grassy shoulder and rested her forehead on the steering wheel.

"I'd never admit this to anyone but you," she murmured, "but I feel as if that beefy Sheila rearranged half my face. Terrible."

Brig slid close and took her in his arms. She gingerly leaned into the comforting embrace. "It's all right to be needy."

"No, it's not," she corrected. "But I can't help myself right now."

"I'll settle for that. Let me drive."

She sighed and said wryly, "Why not? You're practically a member of the staff. I'll just pretend that you're Paradise Springs' first inmate deputy."

"I shouldn't have barged into things tonight, I know."

Millie patted his chest. "Brig, I wasn't the least surprised." She paused, and her voice dropped huskily. "Thanks."

Back at the jail, they went to the deputies' lounge and opened the freezer section of the refrigerator. Millie retrieved something that looked like a blue beanbag. "Reusable ice pack," she explained.

"Come on." He took her by one hand and led her to his cell. "Home sweet home. Lay down on my bunk."

Her face hurt too bad to argue. Millie stretched out,

the cold bag pressed to her eye. He left for a minute, and when he came back, he carried a soft drink can. A straw protruded from the top. While her good eye watched him in amusement, Brig set the can on her chest and slipped the straw between her lips. He sat down on the bunk, his hip casually touching her thigh.

"Why is it that you always end up taking care of me?" she asked, arching her good brow. "Twice, now. I must be injury prone around you."

"Nah. You just didn't have anybody to watch over you before. You think it's strange to have a shoulder to lean on."

"It is." She frowned as much as her condition would allow. "I'm not certain what to do."

"Lean, love, lean. It's that simple." He grinned for a moment. "I left the door open to the reception area. I'll listen for any phone calls. You rest."

"Hmmm." Grateful, she sipped from the drink, then handed it to him. "Enough."

He finished it in a few swallows, then pressed the can against his knee and crumpled it flat with the movement of one large hand.

Millie smiled wearily. "I love men with strong fingers." As a coy look spread across his face, and as she analyzed her words, she smiled ruefully. "I always manage to get myself in trouble with you."

"And it's wonderful, eh, Melisande?"

"Melisande," she repeated softly. "I thought you weren't going to call me that anymore."

He looked away for a moment, and a muscle worked in his jaw. "Didn't want to. Couldn't help myself. It suits you."

"I wish it did," she said fervently. "I wish I could be tough Millie and delicate Melisande at the same time."

Brig looked at her with a seriousness that made her heart stop. "You were delicate *and* tough tonight. I wanted to carry you out of that trailer and kiss you."

Her stomach dropped in delight and shock. "With my uniform on and a bruised eye?"

"Yes, love." He couldn't resist adding devilishly,

"Though I'd rather you had your uniform off. Your badge might stick me."

She stared at him in silent wonder. "I want you so much," Millie whispered.

A taut, intense look of concentration replaced the teasing expression on his face. His voice was a throaty promise. "You've got me."

"For tonight, at least."

Brig shut his eyes, willing his patience to remain strong. He reached out and gently stroked her cheek. "Why are you so afraid that I'll leave you and never look back?"

She was silent for a moment, struggling inwardly. Her tone was cautious. "My family moved every year from the time I was a baby until Dad retired. I was nineteen then. Nineteen years of leaving friends behind, of moving into new apartments and houses. Nineteen years of always struggling to be self-sufficient so that the transitions would be easier. I want permanent things around me now. A permanent home, permanent relationships."

He cupped her chin in his hand, bent forward, and brushed his mouth across hers. He felt the small shiver of response in her body. "I won't make promises tonight, because you wouldn't believe them," he murmured. "But they're there, Melly, waitin' to be said."

"No," she protested in a troubled tone. "No promises."

Brig braced his arms on either side of her and slowly lifted himself to one knee. He moved to the empty half of the small bunk, then lowered himself. Trembling, Millie turned her head on the pillow and looked at him. She sensed his restraint and saw the intensity in his eyes. His breath touched her lips, and a sweet sense of certainty flooded her.

She tilted her head close to his and kissed the corner of his mouth. A rebuking inner voice told her that she should only kiss him briefly, just long enough to sample the texture and taste of his lips. But he moaned, a low, encouraging, masculine sound that unraveled all her good intentions. Millie pushed the ice pack away, and it fell to the floor beside the bed. Her hand crept forward and stroked his jaw while her mouth pressed tighter to his. He opened his lips and welcomed the gentle pressure of her tongue.

Brig shifted and slipped his arms around her, gathering her close to his body. It was natural and easy for her to turn on her side and nestle against the hard length of his torso, feeling her breasts flatten against his chest, feeling his thighs brush hers. He caressed the small of her back, then ran his hands over her hips and pulled them snugly to his own.

Millie exhaled softly, pleasure in the sound, and he captured her breath with a kiss that turned her boneless. The hot, stroking intimacy of his tongue made her want him desperately, and her body arched into the straining hardness between his thighs.

He drew back, his face flushed and eyes groggy, then raised one hand and gently traced the bruise on her left eye. Millie made an inarticulate sound of affection at the way his fingertips eased the pain. "Prize-fighter," he murmured, "you won me."

Brig lifted his head and lightly touched his lips to the bruise, then licked the skin with infinite care. When he passed his tongue over her swollen eyelid, Millie gripped his shoulders and shivered.

"Hurt?" he whispered.

"Just the opposite."

Smiling, he put one hand between their bodies and began unbuttoning her shirt. "Upset you?" he asked.

She laughed helplessly. "Just the opposite."

When his hand delved into the open shirt and slipped under her bra, he inquired, "Too much?"

"Just the opposite."

Grinning now, he slid down and placed a kiss on the top of the breast he cupped in one hand. He pushed the bra strap and shirt off her shoulder, then circled her nipple with his tongue. "Want more?" he asked, his voice a rough whisper. "Don't you *dare* say—"

"More."

His breath exploded in soft chuckles against her sensitive skin, then caught short as he turned his attention to her breasts again. Brig eased her onto her back and took her shirt and bra off. Millie heard roaring in her ears as the cool air added its caress to her body. She moved languidly, trapped in primitive sensations and the hunger of Brig's gaze. He drew his fingertips across her breasts almost reverently, and Millie felt weightless as she watched his eyes move over her.

"I haven't got anything near as pretty as these to show," he said gruffly.

She smiled. "Oh, I suspect that you have something I'd find just as appealing."

He bent his head and took her breasts in his palms, running his thumbs across her nipples, igniting pleasure throughout her body. Then his mouth teased her, nibbling, pulling, until she made wild little sounds and sank her fingers into his hair.

"Tonight is just for you," he whispered as he trailed kisses up her throat. He looked down at her with hooded eyes, knowing that she was vulnerable, that she'd do whatever he asked, but duty and conscience would haunt her later. No, he'd have to wait until he was a free man, and they were someplace besides a jail cell, before he could finish what they'd begun here. Oh, but what a beginning.

Brig undid her trousers and the thick, black belt she wore, then slid his hand inside. She trembled and a mixture of desire and confusion colored her eyes. "Be needy," he urged. "Just lay still and need my touch."

Reassured, she put her hands above her head. Brig curved one hand around them and she gripped tightly. His other hand sought the warm secrets between her thighs. When he cupped her softness, she thought she'd die if he didn't give her more. Affection and passion combined inside her until she wanted to cry out that she loved him. That amazing thought was lost in her passion, and she had no time to analyze it.

"Melisande," he whispered into her ear. "Melisande, I'm going to touch you inside." She moaned as he made good on his words. "That's right, love. Move against my hand. Does this make your eye feel better?"

Confused, dazzled, lost amidst sensation, she chuckled weakly and her voice was barely audible. "What eye?" And then she said his name in a way that made his hips arch against her reflexively.

"Aw, Melly, you could ruin me with a tone like that," he said in a raspy voice.

Brig kissed the parted sweetness of her mouth and groaned when she gave back the pleasure with abandon. His fingers continued to stroke her, slowly, expertly, making her rise and quiver under their guidance.

She twisted her mouth away and drew a long, shuddering breath. Then her eyes settled on his, and he watched her expression as control slipped away. She writhed as sensation washed over her, and Brig shuddered when he felt her wild tremors. She clung to him, shaking with pleasure, and tears came to his eyes.

This was love, then, he thought, this being so happy for Melisande that he didn't mind the unslaked need throbbing in his own body. He gathered her close to him, stroked her golden hair, and kissed her forehead.

"Your needs," she finally managed. "Poor you."

"Sssh. 'Poor me' is about as bloomin' ecstatic as a man can get. Funny thing, eh? Not very macho, eh?"

"Eh," she agreed. "I adore you."

"See there?" His voice was hoarse, his throat tight. "See what bein' sensitive can do for a man? Gets him adored."

"I adore you even when you're not sensitive."

"You mean I've wasted my time studyin' Phil Donahue?"

They both laughed softly. She winced a little, and he got up to retrieve the ice pack. After he put it on her eye, he helped her dress. She watched him with a devotion that made his chest ache with pleasure. Brig covered her with a blanket, then pulled a chair beside the bunk and sat down.

"Sleep for a little while, love," he told her, his hand caressing her hair possessively.

"Can't. I'm on duty."

"Then I'll call Raybo and tell him you're hurt. He'll send somebody to take over."

"I don't ask for favors."

"Melisande, the situation wouldn't be any different if you were a male deputy. Relax."

"The reason I'm accepted around here is that I don't have to ask for help."

"Wrong, love. You're good with people and capable of handlin' anything that comes along. That doesn't mean you have to be tougher than everybody else. Sssh, now. I'll wake you up if anybody calls."

She struggled silently for a moment, then gave him a wistful look. "Promise?"

"Word of honor." He smiled. "That's more serious than swearin' on a kangaroo's hop."

Millie sighed at the gentle sound of his voice and the soothing pressure of his fingers. Her eyes closed, and as she drifted off she felt a deeper sense of peace than she'd ever known in her life.

Dread gnawed at Millie's stomach as she opened her eyes. And then, as her good eye squinted in the sunlight pouring onto her face through the jail cell's window, she knew. Brig had let her sleep past the end of her shift.

"Dammit, no!" Millie threw the blanket off and rolled out of his bunk, ignoring the dull throb that had taken over the left side of her face. She ran to the cell's little dresser and stared at herself in the mirror. Her eye was a rainbow array of colors, heavily favoring the purples, while the rest of her face was colorless.

"I look like a vampire on a day pass," she muttered. She raked her fingers through her hair but it still looked as though it had been combed in a tornado. Her uniform was wrinkled and her shirt hung out of her pants. She had been weak last night, weak and soft and vulnerable, and she looked it. The terrifying part was that she'd enjoyed herself.

Millie straightened her clothes as best she could, then squared her shoulders and went to the lobby. Brig lay on the couch there, reading the morning newspaper. His feet were bare, and he had propped them atop one of the couch's armrests. Charlie sat behind the desk with his feet—not bare, thankfully—propped on a trashcan. He was sipping coffee and listening to a talk show on the radio.

As soon as Brig saw her, he got up hurriedly. "How's the eye, love?"

"What time is it?" she demanded.

"Eight-fifteen," Charlie answered.

Her jaw set, she gazed at Brig angrily. "You promised to wake me up."

"If anyone called. Nobody did."

"My shift ended two hours ago!"

Swinging about stiffly, she walked to the counter and faced Charlie. "I apologize," she told him, her voice clipped. "It won't happen again."

Charlie gave her a slow-eyed blink that made him look like a bewildered bear. "What's wrong, Millie?"

"I'll put the details of the incident on my shift report, and you note on yours that I was asleep in a prisoner's bunk when you got here."

"Melly, stop it," Brig said, his voice grating.

Charlie gaped at her. "I don't want to report you," he said plaintively. "I'm not upset."

Her chin up, she told him, "It's a matter of duty and pride."

"And foolishness," Brig interjected.

Millie did an about-face that was nearly military in execution. He glared down at her in exasperation. "I should have known you'd treat me this way after last night," she declared. "But I'm not a frail little crybaby. I don't need special attention."

"You need to have your fanny paddled."

"Get an army, McKay. If you try it, you'll need help."

When he was upset, he reverted to a heavier accent. His eyes flashed. "I've never walloped a Sheila in me life, so don't strain yerself makin' threats. But bein' that you're such a violent little thing, a good paddlin' is probably the best way to communicate with you!"

"Your true colors are showing," she retorted. "You wanted to play Sir Galahad last night, and in a moment of extreme stupidity, I let you. My mistake. Now you think I'm a helpless little girl who has to be pampered. That may make *you* happy, but it won't work for me."

Millie looked at the hard planes of his face and wondered how she could have seen so much tenderness there last night. He was furious. "You *are* a little girl," he told her. "Because a grown woman has sense enough and grace enough to accept a man's love without thinkin' that he's manipulative and selfish."

"Geez," Charlie said in an awed tone. "Everybody said there was something goin' on between you two, but I didn't believe it."

That was the final blow. Millie pressed her fingers to her temples. Despite all her efforts to maintain a professional appearance, people were gossiping about her and Brig. Whether the gossip was ugly or not didn't matter—a woman who worked at a job traditionally held by men couldn't allow herself any slack. She'd learned that in the navy. When she recalled how Brig's intimate touch had made her forget her responsibilities, she felt like crying.

Millie twisted, walked over to the desk counter, and thumped a fist down. Charlie jumped. "No matter what anyone says, I've never compromised my duty as a deputy. Understand?"

"Nobody said that, Millie, and—"

"And I will never compromise my duty." She jerked a thumb toward Brig. "He's just another prisoner."

Brig crossed his arms over his chest. "One you happen to love."

She whirled around and stared at him. He read anger and shock in her expression, but also a kind of wistful distress that tugged on his heart. Her voice low, she bit into each word as if it were hard. "Are you determined to ruin my professional reputation?"

He didn't miss a beat. "If that's what it takes to teach you a lesson." Brig wouldn't have believed that he'd ever see fear in her beautiful green eyes, but he saw it now. He added, "Lucky for you that I don't kiss and tell."

Her face grim, she went behind the counter, opened a drawer in one of the file cabinets along the back wall, and retrieved her small straw purse. Looking worried, Charlie got up and hovered over her like a mother hen.

"You okay, Millie?"

"Fine. Have a good day."

She came out of the desk area and stopped in front of Brig, gazing up at him with a cold, troubled expression. "I'm going to sit down with Raybo tomorrow and tell him what's happened between you and me. Then I'm giving him my resignation."

For just an instant, Brig looked stunned. Then his eyes narrowed and he said, "Good. It'll make it easier for you to move to Nashville with me."

Her good eye widened in disbelief. Brig was a hard-headed, overconfident, unstoppable freight train of a man. She could either give up, punch him squarely in the face, or laugh. Laughing seemed the best alternative.

Millie cupped a hand over her mouth. Her shoulders shaking, she turned and marched toward the door. It was only when she was outside in the bright July sunshine that she realized how anguished her laughter had sounded.

Six

Raybo sat across from her, graying hair ruffled, paunch a little paunchier from the huge barbecue lunch he'd recently eaten, long legs crossed. He smiled his sweetest good-old-boy smile.

"I'll accept your resignation when hell freezes over," he drawled cheerfully.

Out of sight below the level of his desk, Millie's hands wadded wrinkles into the skirt of her flowered dress. "I don't intend to bring gossip down on you or your office. Can't you see what's going to happen if I keep working around Brig?"

"Millie, folks have always talked about you. This is nothin' new. Different fuel, same fire."

Her breath shortened and she slid to the edge of her chair. "What do you mean?"

Raybo blanched a little. "You don't know?" She shook her head numbly. He sat up, fumbled for her letter of resignation, threw it in the trash, and cleared his throat. "You live so durned far out in the woods and keep to yourself so much that you don't hear much of anything, I reckon."

"That's right. What do people say about me?"

Raybo flung his hands out in a gesture of dismissal. "Same things they'd say about any unmarried woman doin' the kind of work you do. That you don't like men. Or the opposite—that you're one of those women who gets a jolt out of dominatin' men."

Millie relaxed a little. "Oh, that. It comes with the territory."

"Frankly, the rumors about you and Brig McKay are doin' you more good than harm."

"*What*?"

"Well, the folks who think you don't like men have decided that you do, and the folks who think you like to dominate men figure they were wrong, 'cause Brig wouldn't take after a woman who tried to do that. So all in all, he's the best thing that ever happened to your reputation."

Millie slumped back in her chair. "Good grief."

"You gonna run off with him?"

She straightened again. "No!"

"Why not?"

She sighed. "It wouldn't last. I'm a sexy little challenge to him right now, but what would I be to him in Nashville? A weapon's expert with martial arts' skills and a penchant for whacking people, that's what."

"A man can always use a woman like that," Raybo said hopefully.

"Or he can try to change her, and when he can't, he can tell her good-bye." Millie struggled for a moment with the lump in her throat and tried to sound nonchalant. "I hate good-byes. Guess it comes from all those years of leaving people behind when my family moved."

Raybo sighed and picked up a document on his desk. "You better start gettin' ready for this one then. Judge up in Nashville says to let Brig go a week from today. Early release for good behavior."

"I'm gonna be *what* in a week?" Brig asked incredulously.

"Free," Raybo repeated.

Brig, who sat on the edge of his bunk, put his head

in his hands and cursed soundly. "I've gotta have more than a week."

"I know it's a horrible thing to do you, son," Raybo said dryly. "That Nashville judge must be mean as hell."

Brig stood up and paced, his hands on his hips. "Does Melisande know?"

"Yep."

"I'll talk to her as soon as she comes back from her day off."

"She's not coming back, son."

Brig stopped pacing. "I thought you said she didn't resign."

"She didn't. But she took vacation time for the rest of the week. Said she thought it'd be best to stay clear of you. Gal's as spooked as a bird in a hailstorm."

Brig cursed again, rammed a hand through his hair, and turned toward Raybo in supplication. He was desperate for time, and Millie was running like hell. "All right, this calls for imagination."

Raybo smiled sweetly. "Son, on that count I reckon I can help you."

Millie wasn't in the mood for problems. She had enough of them already, considering the fact that Brig would be out of jail in a few days. With him a free man, able to roam where he wanted and confront her at will, she'd have no peace.

So when she came home from the grocery store one morning and found a hole where a young magnolia tree had stood in her front yard an hour earlier, her tension exploded and she swore revenge.

Millie ran into the cottage and came back with a loaded shotgun. With the shotgun tucked under the convertible's front seat, she spun gravel out to the main road and raced to the tiny clapboard house a half-mile away.

The house sat less than two-dozen yards back from the road, a relic from the time when the road was nothing but a sandy trail. Just as Millie had expected, Imogene Berkley, ninety-five years old but still keen enough to spit tobacco at a fly and hit it, sat rocking on the front porch.

"Miss Imogene, did you see anybody go by hauling a magnolia tree?" Millie yelled from the car.

A nod. A bony black finger pointed north. A stream of tobacco arched over the edge of the porch and hit a sluggish yellow tabby cat in the head. " 'Bout ten minutes ago."

"Bless your heart!"

"Your tree?"

"Yes!"

Miss Imogene rocked faster. Someone had stolen all her azaleas a month before. "Kill 'em." More tobacco juice leapt through the air. The cat ducked this time.

Millie liked Miss Imogene's attitude. She gave her a whimsical salute and drove away.

She felt as proud as a mother cat about to take a particularly tasty dinner home to her kittens. Everyone would be so proud. Especially Brig.

"Keep it still or I'll shoot it off, scum," Millie told the slack-jawed redhead wearing overalls. She poked her shotgun into the chest of the similarly slack-jawed blond. "You too, slime-for-brains." The two men sat on the office floor at Perkle Greenhouse and Nursery where they'd tried to sell her tree. Their hands and feet were bound with baling wire and construction tape, courtesy of Henry Perkle. Henry lounged nearby, grinning.

"Miss Millie, you sure you aren't half tiger and half greyhound?"

Millie looked down at her mud-stained blue jeans and torn T-shirt. She'd run the tree-stealing Roger boys around the nursery grounds a few times before she'd cornered them, appropriately, behind a manure pile. She chuckled. "I think I'm half warthog and half skunk."

"Then you're a credit to your species," Henry noted.

The sound of a siren signaled the arrival of Charlie and the patrol car. After a stunned assessment of what she'd accomplished, Charlie grinned at her affectionately, put a ham-like hand on the back of the Roger brothers' necks, and guided them to the car.

Millie got back in her old convertible and followed Charlie to the jail. A sleek black limousine sat in the parking lot. "Who hired the hearse?" Millie asked, as she and Charlie prodded the Roger boys out of the patrol car.

"Don't know." Excited, he went over and peered into the front window.

"I'll take our green-thumbed friends on into the jail," Millie called. After all, the Roger boys were her collar, even if she was off duty. She wanted to show them off. They shuffled along as best they could, considering that their feet were still tied. Poking their backs with her shotgun, she herded them up the steps and through the front doors.

Raybo leaped up from the desk and hurried toward her, then gave a happy whoop. Millie beamed at him, her chest swelling with anticipation. "Nothing to it," she began. "I was on them like a duck on a June bug."

"Natty Brannigan is here!" he interrupted.

Millie halted. "What's a Natty Brannigan?"

"Best new country-western entertainer of last year! Haven't you ever heard "You Calling Me Unfaithful Is Like the Pot Calling the Kettle Black"? It won a Grammy!"

"Lovely," Millie said in a dry tone. "And she's visiting Brig, I suppose."

"Yep. She's the one Brig fought over in Nashville."

Millie smiled sickly. She remembered now. "How nice." Depression settled in her stomach, but she tried to carry on. "I just closed down a plant-theft operation that covered five counties." She gestured toward her unhappy-looking prisoners. "May I present Arnold and Malcolm Rogers."

"Yeah, go put 'em in a cell." Raybo went to the check-in desk and picked up the phone. "I gotta call the newspaper and tell 'em that Natty Brannigan is here."

Millie succumbed to a sense of defeat as she guided her prisoners into the cell block. Brig's cell was empty. Tilting her head toward the closed door to the recreation room, she wondered if Brig and Natty Brannigan were in there. She vaguely recalled seeing a photograph of the woman.

Great lips. That's what the woman had. Pouting, bee-stung lips. And oh, yes, great eyes, that could make a man forget to breathe. The woman was a debutante, the daughter of a former governor. The woman was tall and willowy. The woman had earned Brig's affection so much that he'd taken a two-month jail term for defending her. He had refused to tell the judge and jury what the fight was about. Gallant, that was Brig.

"Get in that cell," Millie demanded, pointing the slow-moving Roger brothers through an open door. Arnold, the blond, twisted around and leered at her.

"I'm not goin' in. How do you like that, you butch little bitch?" he asked smoothly.

She fought repulsion. "How do I like that?" she repeated, her voice rising. The anguish inside her boiled over. "*How* do I like that?" She grabbed his collar and yelled, "Didn't anybody warn you about the tough lady deputy? Didn't they tell you that I'm violent? For all you know, I could have PMS!"

Arnold's eyes widened and he took a step back. She took a step forward, screwing her face into a fiercer expression as she did. "I didn't mean nothin'," Arnold mumbled.

"Sure you did! And now you're going to pay! Sometimes I get so mad I have to be restrained! *Restrained*, Arnold, but right now there's no one here to restrain me!"

Malcolm, who had shuffled to the far side of the cell, threw back his head and screamed, "Help! She's gonna hurt my brother!"

"Get in that cell with Malcolm, Arnold!"

"Okay! Okay!" Arnold took baby steps backward, his feet shifting frantically to compensate for their bindings.

The door from the recreation room banged open. "What the hell's going on in here?"

Millie swung around at the sound of Brig's deep voice. The tall, elegant, and delicate Natty Brannigan stood behind him, clutching his arm and peering over his shoulder. She had hair like brown silk.

"Close that door, Mr. McKay, and mind your own business!"

"Strewth. Melisande. What are you doin'?"

He strode forward. Millie ran out of the cell, slammed the door, and held up a warning hand. "This isn't your concern. Take your friend back into the recreation room or I'll order her out of the jail."

He halted, exasperated, and put his hands on his hips. "Dammit, you look as if you've been chasin' pigs through a sty. Are you all right?"

Humiliation fueled new anger in her. Natty Brannigan was spell-binding in high heels and a creamy, flowing dress. If words could wound, then Brig had just scored a direct hit. "Thank you so much for telling me how bad I look," Millie said with slow, lethal precision. "I'm fine."

He exhaled in dismay. "Dammit, don't misinterpret my words. Melisande, meet Natalie Brannigan. Natty, meet Melisande. Melisande, Natty came down from Nashville to talk to you. She was comin' out to your place in a little while."

"Why? Looking for a bodyguard? With a body like yours, Ms. Brannigan, you need an army of them. And I mean that as a compliment."

Natty spoke up. In a voice born of magnolias and money, she said firmly, "Now listen, honey, there isn't any ol' reason for you to get yourself fidgety. I just want to tell you a few things about Brig here."

"I gotta go to the john!" Arnold called to Millie. "You'd better untie my hands."

Millie saw anger replace exasperation on Brig's face. Arnold was about to get a different kind of attention than he bargained for. "How's about I fix it so you don't ever have to go to the john again?" he asked Arnold.

"Police brutality!" Malcolm yelled.

Raybo came into the cell block. "Can't a man use the phone without a damned circus in the background?" He faced Millie and jabbed a finger at her. "Do you have this situation under control?"

She was dying inside. It didn't matter that she wasn't even on duty or wearing a uniform. She was responsible. "Yes, sir."

"Then make it sound that way!"

"Yes, sir."

As he stomped off, she turned back toward Brig. She didn't care that his gaze centered immediately on the sheen of tears she couldn't hide. Having tears in her eyes was one thing. Letting them fall was another. Her brother Kyle had once called her "Clint Eastwood with boobs". Clint wouldn't cry if his dignity were going belly up, and neither would she.

"I don't have anything to say to you," she told Brig. "And I don't want my arm twisted by your old girlfriend. I grant you one thing, you inspire loyalty among your women."

"Well, I declare," Natty said. You sure have got the situation wrong."

"Spare me the Scarlett O'Hara act."

Charlie hurried into the cell block, huffing. "Sorry, Mel. Didn't mean to stay outside so long. I'll take over."

"Melisande," Brig interjected, looking upset and worried. "Come on into the rec room and talk with me and Natty."

"I have paperwork to fill out." Millie propped her shotgun on one shoulder. She watched Natty's amused eyes go over her and the gun as if both were from a bad horror movie: *Petite Deputies From Hell*.

Brig shook his head. "Melisande, don't be stubborn."

"Stow it," she retorted.

His eyes turned dark with anger. "Hellion."

Millie nodded, while her heart twisted into a large lump of suffering. His ex-lover was standing behind him, aflutter with grace and elegance and traditional femininity. Why had he thought that meeting Natty Brannigan would reassure her in some way? It only confirmed Millie's fear that she wouldn't fit into his life. She had no doubts now. No doubts, no hope, and no control left. Turning on one heel, she left the cell block quickly.

Brig slapped his hand against one thigh and, for Natty's sake, fought back several vicious words.

"Sorry, Brig," Charlie said wistfully. "Guess plan one didn't work."

Natty cleared her throat and patted Brig's arm. "I would have talked some sense into the little thing, if she'd given me half a chance."

Brig sighed. "I know, Natty, I know."

"She certainly is spunky."

He laughed wearily. Spunky, yes. Now if he could just come up with some way to get Spunky to quit running, before time ran out on them both.

He was gone, and the cell felt like a cell again.

Millie sat on the bare mattress of Brig's empty bunk. She gazed at the spot on the dresser where he'd always thrown his ridiculous, macho bush hat. She looked at the corner chair where he'd always left his guitar.

"Feels kind of lonesome without him here," Suds commented from the cell door.

Millie stood up slowly, noting that her body and spirit seemed to be about two-hundred years old this morning. "I should put one of the Roger brothers in here."

"No. Wouldn't be right."

After a moment, she nodded. "It'd be like putting a mule in a thoroughbred's stall."

"Yes."

"He took a hotel suite in town?"

"Yes. Millie, I'm sure he'll come to see you."

She went to the cell's window and stood with her back to Suds so that he wouldn't see her tears. "I hope not."

Millie forced herself to stay busy, but the day passed in lethargic routine. She wondered where Brig was. She wondered how many nights she'd cry before she washed him out of her memory enough to get on with her life. She wondered how it would have been to make love to him, to sleep with him, to watch him smile when he woke up in the morning.

About four-thirty, a monster of a man walked into the lobby and towered over her desk. Millie looked up in awe, then noted the pleasant, somewhat dull look on his beefy face.

"Hi," he boomed. He raised both hands in mock menace and growled. "Name's George Oliver. But you can call me Killer Cretin. I'm a wrestler."

Millie laughed. "What can I do for you?"

"I got lost. Which way to the Happy Mac?"

The Happy Mac was a small blue-collar bar. "Go back to the main road and take a left. It's just over five miles. On the right."

"Geez. I'm late. Thanks for the info." He growled again, and left.

Charlie arrived for the shift change just as the call came from the Happy Mac bar. Millie took notes, then sat frowning at them for a minute.

"What's up?" Charlie asked.

"Brig's fighting. He's fighting with someone at the Happy Mac bar." She began to shake with disbelief and fury. "How *could* he! He'll blow his parole!"

"Want me to take the call?"

"No. I'm going to strangle him."

She was out the door in five seconds.

The Happy Mac bar sat just off the road in a grove of spindly pine trees. In the chic world of Paradise Springs, it was a beer-and-pretzels hangout where sweat-stained men threw their hard hats at each other and argued lustily about sports. But it was a homey place, and the time Millie had gone there to drink a beer with Charlie and Suds, she'd felt welcome and comfortable.

Her heart pounding, Millie walked into the dimly lit bar and surveyed the wreckage of broken tables and smashed glasses. More than a dozen men lounged around, looking as if they'd just been royally entertained.

Brig sat at one of the few unharmed tables, his booted feet extended in front of him and crossed at the ankles, his hands resting nonchalantly on his thighs. Killer Cretin, alias George Oliver, sat beside him.

The bar's owner stood behind them both, a pistol leveled at their heads.

"Evenin', Melisande," Brig said cheerfully.

"Don't look so calm." She heard her voice tremble with disappointment and despair. "Are you crazy? What in the world is wrong with you?"

He shrugged. He wore jeans and the white polo shirt he'd had on when he arrived in Paradise Springs, only now the shirt had a huge rip across the chest. A trickle of blood stained one corner of his mouth. George looked disheveled, but almost sleepy.

Millie took a deep breath. "What happened, Bill?" she asked the owner.

"McKay picked a fight with this gorilla. I thought they were going to kill each other, and they busted the crap outta my place."

Millie leveled a hard gaze at Brig, but found nothing but quiet scrutiny in his blue eyes. "Why?" she asked, her throat tight.

"I like to fight, love."

"You're on parole! You know that! Are you so thoughtless that you didn't consider the consequences?"

"It's my own life."

"Right," she said sardonically. Millie rubbed her forehead. "Bill, if Mr. McKay pays damages, will you forget about pressing charges?"

"I don't want any special treatment," Brig said. "If he doesn't press charges, I won't pay the damages."

"Crazy Aussie bastard," Bill said. "If that's how he wants it, that's how he's got it."

Millie felt as if she might be sick. She gazed at Brig through narrowed eyes. "I never considered you a fool before. Brawling for fun is one thing, but risking your parole was just plain stupid."

"Be quiet, Melly, and do your job."

His reserved, almost taunting attitude whipped at her. She pulled out a set of handcuffs and motioned with her hand. For one instant, she wanted to turn and simply walk out of the bar. This felt wrong, so wrong. She didn't want to do this to him.

"Up, McKay."

He unfolded his athletic frame from the chair and stood, then put his hands out, waiting. Struggling for composure, Millie snapped the cuffs into place. Her skin felt like the cover of a drum, and she could tell that a massive headache was coming on. Millie nodded toward George Oliver.

"Bill? This guy was just defending himself."

"That's right," George noted, and yawned.

"Are you going to press charges?"

"Hell, yes," the bar's owner said.

George's brows arched. All lassitude gone, he sat bolt upright in his chair. "Hey. It wasn't my fault."

"You looked like you were enjoying it," the owner sniffed. "I'm pressing charges."

"No need for that, mate," Brig interjected. "It was my fight."

"I don't care!" The owner looked at Millie and jerked his thumb toward George. "Arrest both of them!"

George held up both hands and gazed at Brig in protest. "I didn't bargain for this, man!"

Millie squinted at him in bewilderment. "Bargain for what, Killer?"

"Quiet, Killer," Brig intoned.

"What, Killer?"

George gulped. "McKay, help me out! I got a family! I live around here! I don't want a jail record!"

Brig sighed, then cursed under his breath. He twisted around to face Millie. "Don't haul him off. I paid him to fight. I wanted to break my parole so I could go back to jail."

"This boy spent too many years in the Australian heat," Bill commented.

Millie felt her knees go weak. "You'd give up a month of your precious freedom?" she asked hoarsely.

Brig nodded. He wasn't going to embarrass her in front of the two men, so he didn't explain anything more. But she knew. He was willing to give up a month of freedom so that he could be close to her. Freedom was vital to him. He'd told her so. She knew how great a sacrifice he was offering.

Her eyes burning, she looked toward the owner. "You can't press charges against Mr. Oliver," she told him. "It's not fair." After a moment, he nodded. "And you can be sure that Mr. McKay will pay the damages, so you don't have to press charges against him."

"That's not how I want it," Brig said grimly. "No argument. I'm going back to jail."

"All I want is my damages!" Bill yelled.

"You'll get 'em, mate. Soon as you file charges."

Millie gave Brig a despairing look. Underneath his laid-back exterior was a nature as stubborn as her own. "Don't do this. Please," she said gruffly, begging him with her eyes. "No one deserves this kind of sacrifice."

Her meaning was clear. Brig answered in the same tone. "I'd rather give up my freedom than leave town alone."

Tenderness. Passion. Devotion. Millie felt all three with an intensity that shocked her. She knew suddenly that to be wanted by this man was a blessing. Every moment she spent with him could only enrich her life, and even if their time together didn't last, she'd count herself lucky to have been cherished by him. A sense of certainty brought enormous peace to her.

She smiled calmly and nodded. "If that's the way you want it, Brig, let's go."

He gave her abrupt change of mood a quizzical frown, but said nothing. She put one small hand on his brawny forearm and guided him out of the bar. He got into the patrol car's backseat, and she shut the door behind him. The bar's owner came outside, and Millie told him she'd be back the next morning to write up the paper-work.

She drove away without glancing at Brig and began to hum.

"You don't have to sound so happy about things, love," he grumbled.

"I'm not the one locked in the back of a patrol car with my hands cuffed. Why shouldn't I be happy?"

"I know you don't care about me the way I care about you, but you can make it less damned obvious."

"Is that how you interpret humming? My, you're oversensitive."

"I don't expect you to fall at my feet and worship, but a little appreciation would be nice."

"You mean because you broke up a bar on my be-half? It's not too late to convince the owner to drop the charges."

"Hell, no. I'm stayin' in your jail where I can do my best to seduce you. I'm gonna ruin you for any other man. I'm gonna turn you inside out until you can't think of anything but doin' what I tell you to do."

"Whew!" She grinned. "What confidence."

"What drivin'. You just missed the turnoff to the jail."

"I know."

"Where are you draggin' me off to?"

"I've sold you into slavery. A wealthy widow in Miami wants to add you to her harem. She has a thing for men with Aussie accents and bad tempers."

"Melisande," he said warningly.

"It's a surprise." She chuckled. "A surprise by Sur-prise."

"I'm goin' to jail. I *won't* change my mind, no matter what you do to me."

"Oh, yes, you will."

He swore colorfully and asked questions, none of which she answered. A few minutes later Millie steered the patrol car into her own driveway. When they reached the cottage, she got out, opened the back door, and motioned to Brig.

"Move it, McKay."

His eyes were alight with intrigue as he maneuvered out of the seat. "What the hell?"

"Quiet. Do as you're told. Into the house." He eyed her askance but headed for the front door. Millie opened it and waved him inside. He stopped in the living room and she prodded his back. "Keep going."

"Where?"

"Bedroom."

A disbelieving half-smile began to ease the hardness from his expression. "Oh." He strode into the bedroom with her right behind him. "What now?"

"Sit on the side of the bed."

He did as she ordered. The room was shadowy and cool. The air vibrated with anticipation. "Melisande, what are you gonna do with me?" he asked gruffly, and the tone of his voice made it obvious that he wouldn't protest.

Her eyes glowing, she knelt in front of him and gently took his face between her small, strong hands. "You're my prisoner, now," she whispered.

Seven

Brig quivered at the soft touch of her fingers caressing his jaw and the adoration gleaming in her green eyes. He raised his face toward heaven and said heartily, "Thank you, Mate."

She melted with laughter and desire. "Brig. Oh, Brig." Millie nestled between his knees and rested her head against his chest.

"You're not just doin' this because you feel sorry for any man crazy enough to do what I did today?" His voice was husky.

She tilted her head back and gazed at him raptly. Millie brought one hand to her mouth, wet the fingertips with her tongue, then began wiping away the dried blood at the corner of his lips. He exhaled softly, affected by her technique.

"I don't feel sorry for you," she murmured. "I feel sorry for coldhearted, lonely little Millie Surprise."

Brig twisted his head and kissed her palm. "Why?"

"Because I don't know how I've lived twenty-nine years without you."

Another shudder ran through him. His shoulders flexed against the restraint of the handcuffs. "Undo me, Melisande, and we'll both find out what we've been missin'."

With a little cry of pleasure, she rose slightly and pressed her mouth to his. They traded a desperate, almost violent kiss as she fumbled for the cuff key in a pocket of her trousers.

"Wait," she urged.

" 'Wait' isn't part of my vocabulary right now."

She kissed him quickly, sucking the tip of his tongue as he thrust forward, trying to snare her for another long moment. "Wait," she said again.

"Woman, I've waited for weeks!"

Millie unlocked the cuffs. The metal contrivance slid off the bed and landed on the floor with a rattle. Brig quickly held out his arms.

"Com'ere, Melisande," he ordered hoarsely.

She flung herself at him, giving roughness because it was desired, digging her fingers into his shoulders as he jerked her tightly to him and bent his head to hers. He dragged his fingers down her back and cupped her rump with both hands. She met his mouth with a wantonness that made his fingers squeeze her rhythmically. She had only one mission in the world, and that was to pleasure him and be pleasured in return.

They fell back on the bed together, with one of his long legs curved possessively over her lower body. He slid both arms around her as she raised her face to his hungry mouth. In between kisses he muttered lightly, "Ow. Ow. Hell. Ow. It stuck me. I knew it."

"What?"

"Your badge, love." He laughed, and the deep sound sent delicious shivers skating across her stomach.

Millie tucked her chin and gazed at the area where his chest pressed snuggly to her own. "I think we need fewer dangerous clothes between us."

He snaked a hand into her hair and tilted her head back. For a moment he trailed kisses along the curve of her throat, making inarticulate sounds of happiness when he heard her moan.

"Please tell me that you're off duty," he deadpanned.

"I'm all yours until morning."

"And then?" He looked at her with the hunger of a man anticipating a feast.

She whimpered at the thought of sharing that feast. "I'll have to go back to work."

"Oh." He gave her a slow, devastating smile. "I thought you meant something important. But work's okay. You go, I'll wait for you to come back."

"In bed?" she whispered.

"In bed." His voice dropped to a sexy rumble. "Naked and ready. Waitin' for you to come home from work tomorrow."

She moved reflexively at the idea, her hips rising against the weight of his leg. His eyes darkened and he buried his face in her neck, nibbling. "But let's not get ahead of ourselves, love. We've got a lot of naked-and-ready to take care of today." He lifted his head suddenly and frowned. "What about returnin' the patrol car?"

Millie sank her fingers into his hair and stroked lazily. "I should call Charlie right now and tell him that I'm keeping it overnight. Raybo lets the deputies do that occasionally."

Brig reached for the phone on her bedside table. Snatching the receiver up, he held it within her reach. "I want you to get your work chores done and forgotten." His expression was incredibly tender but demanding. "I want you to concentrate on nothing but what I'm gonna do to you."

The breath soughed out of her, and she could only nod blankly. Millie wasn't sure what numbers she punched into the phone. Her attention was riveted to Brig's searing gaze. He put the phone to her ear and began kissing her. Charlie answered.

Millie dragged her mouth away from Brig's and cleared her throat. "Charlie?" she squeaked in something approximating Minnie Mouse's voice. She shut her eyes, took a deep breath, and tried to ignore the muffled sound of Brig's laughter, buried in the bedspread beside her head. "Charlie," she said in a more normal tone. "I took care of the problem at the Happy Mac."

They both heard Charlie's booming voice say, "Where's Brig?"

He and Millie shared a contemplative look. "With me," she said finally. "He's going to pay damages at the bar. There won't be any charges filed. Charlie, I'm keeping the car overnight, if that's all right."

There was silence for a moment. Then there was only the sound of Charlie whooping with glee. Brig smiled and grabbed the phone from her. "G'night, mate!" he yelled cheerfully. Then he slammed the phone back on its base.

"Back to the good stuff," he said with happy lechery.

Millie laughed, feeling delirious. "Oh, boy."

Brig felt the wild trembling of her body as he unbuttoned her shirt, and he reveled in the knowledge that he could create such vivid emotion in a woman who prided herself on control. He drew her shirt open and watched the harsh rise and fall of her chest. Her full breasts strained against the material of her bra. Brig dipped his head and nestled kisses between them.

"Melisande," he said huskily, his lips on her skin. "All I expected was for you to take me back to jail today. After the way you've been holdin' me off, what changed your mind?"

His lips gauged the shiver that ran through her. "I finally admitted to myself that every minute I get with you is precious," she whispered. She feathered one hand over his hair, stroking, while the other hand slid back and forth across the hard terrain of his shoulders. "No matter what happens later, I have to be with you."

"We'll stay together. We're suited to each other." He raised his head and studied her with eyes drenched in tenderness. "I promise."

"Don't promise," she begged in a barely audible voice.

He frowned mildly, then forced himself to nod. "We'll make love, and let the future see to itself."

"Yes."

Her shirt lay open like a vest. Brig braced himself on

one elbow and slid a hand up her quivering stomach. "How do you want me, Melly? Fast or slow? Rough or gentle?"

She moaned. "I didn't know I had so many choices." His large, expert fingers slipped under the flimsy material of her bra and tugged the garment off center. Giving her a strained, devilish little smile, he caressed the breast he'd exposed.

"Speak up," he ordered gruffly.

Her eyes, glazed with emotion, fluttered shut, then opened to squint at him with halfhearted rebuke. "Fast and gentle," she murmured.

The color darkened in his face, giving him a hungry, intense look that was purely masculine and highly erotic. "I hoped you'd say that."

He hurriedly removed her shirt and bra, tossing them to the floor. She gripped his torn polo shirt and pulled it over his head. Millie ran her hands down his chest, enjoying the luxurious contrast of hair and hard muscle. "Did Killer Cretin hurt you?"

"Will you kiss every spot that aches?" She nodded, smiling. He rolled onto his back. "Here." Brig pointed to the center of his chest.

"Poor baby," she crooned. Her heart racing, Millie bent her head over his naked torso and lapped at the spot with her tongue, then pressed a damp kiss to it. His back arched slightly, and she let her gaze trail down to his jean-covered hips. The symbol of his readiness made a large and impatient hill in the flat expanse of his groin.

She reached out slowly and covered it with her hand. "Does this ache?" she whispered.

He shuddered wildly. "Is a crocodile mean?"

"Is this like a crocodile?"

Brig chuckled hoarsely. "It's dangerous, for sure."

Millie planted small kisses down to his navel. He was delightfully hairy, and she loved the uninhibited way he groaned when she nuzzled her nose in the dark fur on his stomach. "I love danger," she assured him, as she unzipped his jeans and touched him. He chuckled, the sound strained. She stretched out beside him, her face burrowed in his shoulder. "That's one magnificent crocodile," Millie noted in an awed tone.

"You're makin' the ache worse, not better." He rolled onto his side, took her in a fierce embrace, and kissed her until she sagged weakly against him.

"I ache too," she managed to say against the heated caress of his lips.

Within seconds he had her stripped naked and trembling under his hand. "You feel like warm cream," he whispered, as his fingers explored intimately. He sank his mouth onto one of her nipples.

Her body's sweet agony played havoc with coherent thought. "F-fast," she reminded him, her hands trying desperately to touch every exposed inch of his chest and arms.

With a growling sound of anticipation he sat up and began tugging at his boots. "I've got to get me toes free."

"Had you planned to use them in some way?"

He stopped long enough to kiss her until she couldn't breathe. "You never know, Melly, you never know."

Laughing helplessly, Millie knelt in front of him and grabbed one boot between her hands. She had always sensed that Brig was the kind of man who'd bring both gentleness and earthy humor to bed. The thought of what they were about to share made her pant lightly. He slung a boot onto the floor and sat still. Millie looked up to find his eyes on her parted lips and flushed, naked body. His expression drew tight, as if in pain.

"What's wrong?" she asked quickly.

He inhaled with a rough sound. "I could lose control just lookin' at you. I've never felt like this before."

She leaned back, tingling all over, her mouth widening into a circle of stunned happiness. Never had she felt so wanted. Never had she felt so wonderfully female.

Her eyes burned with tears of delight. "Make love to me right now, right this second."

He held out one big hand. It was shaking. "Come here."

Brig still wore his jeans and one boot. It didn't matter to either of them as she grasped his hand, and he pulled her onto his lap. She wound her arms around his neck and cried out raggedly as his open jeans allowed his hard flesh to thrust against her, seeking entry.

Brig rolled her onto her back, and she felt the hot, pulsing length of him between her thighs. "Fast," he promised. "But gentle."

That was the way they joined together, her body rising to meet his as he pressed carefully into her sleek, tight welcome. He cupped her head into the crook of his neck, and she kissed his moist skin. Millie inhaled the distinctive scent of him, male flesh, sweat, and arousal.

It sent passionate shivers through her and made her legs struggle to open wider, as if she could take still more of him inside her body. She cupped her feet to the backs of his legs and rode his swift, pounding movements. He gathered her hips in his hands and lifted her to meet his thrusts, then called her name with the broken tone of a man who clung to the last shred of restraint.

That loving sound catapulted her into a dimension where his movements merged with the sensations swirling deep within her womb. Clutching his shoulders, Millie arched her head back and moaned repeatedly as desire exploded in second after second of pleasure.

He raised his head, and through a haze of passion she caught the look in his half-shut eyes—wild, possessive, primitive. The wildness reached out to her like a heated caress, and she writhed under him, losing herself again.

"Oh, love," he groaned, the sound husky and tender. "Take me with you."

He brushed a kiss across her mouth, shuddered violently once, then again. His body bowed over her, and she felt the sensual twist of his lips as pleasure shot through him. For one breathless instant she and he were locked in the stillness of shattering emotion, knowing only each other and the sharing of ecstasy.

Millie's body hummed with a joy so exquisite that it was almost unbearable. She shut her eyes and felt the harsh trembling of Brig's hands as he cupped her face between them. His mouth brushed over her cheeks and forehead, setting off pinpoints of sensation on the tingling skin. He took her lower lip in his teeth and nibbled carefully. Her mouth felt deliciously swollen.

"You taste like sex and love," he whispered. "I've never tasted anything so good." His body relaxed heavily on hers. With a sigh, he lowered his head beside hers and nuzzled her neck.

Millie gloried in the feel of his hot, satiated body pressing firmly into hers, his masculine flesh still inside her and far from soft. His jeans were nearly off his hips, and she managed to draw her legs back far enough to hook her toes into the waistband. With careful little shoves, she pushed his jeans down to his thighs.

He raised his head and gave her a sexy, crooked grin. "Those are fantastic toes you've got. You see? Toes are handy in bed."

She nodded. Millie studied the glowing affection in his eyes and knew that she returned it. Her throat tight with emotion, she whispered, "I love you, Brigand."

His grin faded into a look so serious that she was afraid for a moment. Was her announcement too soon, or too unexpected?

"You realize," he told her in a deep, firm voice, "that this complicates things."

Her eyes widened in concern, and a sinking sensation nudged at her stomach. "I thought you knew. You acted as if you knew."

He nodded, his mouth a tight line. "Oh, I knew. But hearing you admit it makes a difference."

"Why?" she asked, her voice airy.

"Because now I expect you to say it all the time." He lifted a hand and wagged his finger at her in mock warning. "In bed, out of bed, on the telephone, in public . . ."

"You horrible tease!" As relief sleeted through her, she smacked his bare back with the palm of her hand. "I thought you were upset!"

"I'll be upset if you don't say it again!" he yelled boisterously.

Suddenly giddy, she bent her head back and shouted, "I love you!"

"That's 'I love you, *Brig*'!"

She shouted louder. "I love you, Brig!"

His sex was still deep within her. With a gentle thrust, he demonstrated what had been happening to it while they yelled at each other. Millie's back arched, and he chuckled happily as he slid a hand between them to caress her breasts.

She groaned in exaggerated dismay. "You have a way with words, mate."

"Then listen to this." He bent his head next to her ear and murmured in a husky tone, "I love you dearly, Melisande. I've been waitin' all my life for you, you wild little woman." His fingers feathered over one of her taut nipples, spreading the moisture that came from both his skin and hers.

Millie's fingers dug into his shoulders. He moved against her, igniting new desires with every rocking motion of his hips. "Say it again," she ordered huskily.

"I love you." He laced the words with so much tenderness that she cried out. "Now you say it," he told her.

She began to smile. "I *love* you."

He smiled back. Their eyes met and held. There was no more need for words.

So this was life with Brig McKay. Over the next few days he lounged around her cottage, writing songs, talking long-distance about business, watching television. He shocked her by washing dishes and straightening the house, and she realized that he was much neater and more organized than his image made people believe.

And he cooked. Strange concoctions, and hardly good for her waistline, but wonderful. He made stew, or he barbecued ribs on the grill on her back porch, or he built monstrous deli sandwiches with four kinds of meat and two kinds of cheese.

He taught her to pluck a few chords on his guitar, but eventually pronounced her "more beautiful than musical," and took his guitar back. She promised to practice.

And they made love. Sometimes it was so slow and spiritual that they lay in silent, peaceful wonder afterwards. Other times it was as bawdy as a wrestling match—no holds barred, no referee, furniture and clothing beware. In between, they shared the growing, precious knowledge that they enjoyed being quiet together for hours at a time.

Millie's father had donated great-great-great-grandmother Melisande's diary to the state historical society, but he kept a carefully photocopied version for the family. Brig was curious about it. He stretched out on the couch one night, wearing nothing but jeans, and she sat on the floor close enough for his hand to stroke her hair. Millie opened the diary and cleared her throat.

"Melisande wrote about how she and Jacques fell in love. She was amazingly frank. I'm going to paraphrase this, because otherwise you'd have trouble making sense of her grammar. English was her second language, and it shows."

"Have trouble with it meself," Brig commented dryly.

"Your other talents compensate quite well."

He arched a brow wickedly. "Liked me beef log tonight, did you?"

Chuckling, Millie began to read. " 'This great, hulking brute of a man with hair the color of onyx had, by this time, held me prisoner on his ship for ten days. He was so fierce, so determined that I should fear him, that during our first days together I was terrified. But by now, I knew better. I had seen his kindness to his crew; I knew he was honorable, even though he stole me from my wedding.' "

"She didn't want to marry the other guy, right?" Brig interjected.

"Right. It was an arranged marriage. Jacques told her the kidnapping was for revenge—her Spanish fiancé had Jacques' father killed." Millie turned a page in the diary and continued reading. " 'A man without honor would have used me as a man uses a woman, but Jacques St. Serpris did not. From the first night of my capture, when I tried to thank him, he warned me not to stir passions he kept under poor control. I learned later that he made me fear him in order to protect us both. He was a pirate, and I, a lady of genteel means. The two should not blend, *n'est-ce pas*?' "

"Damn, you Surprises are *all* hung up on this incompatibility thing," Brig interjected wryly. "It's a bloody wonder the family survived."

"Be quiet," Millie said, amused. "We manage. Listen to this. 'On my eleventh day with him, his ship was attacked by a Spanish galleon from the West Indies. Jacques shut me in his cabin and gave me a pistol to protect myself. The fighting became fierce outside my door, and I waited with a great deal more bravery than I thought possible. Jacques had taught me to recognize my strengths. When the cabin door burst open, I had my pistol aimed for a killing shot.' "

"Typical Surprise woman," Brig commented. "Shoot first and ask questions later."

"Sssh. 'Jacques stood there, bloody, wounded, barely able to keep to his feet. He had been defending me outside the door. He stared down at me and knew that I could easily take revenge for all the fearsome treatment I'd received from him. But I searched my soul and understood that I had become his prisoner in a new way. When I lowered the gun and went to him, crying out my concern, he was shocked. "I waited for you to kill me," he said. And I answered, "Dear man, would I tear out my own heart?" ' "

Millie lowered the diary and swallowed hard. She gazed at Brig and found his eyes full of fascination. Almost on cue, both of them exhaled. "That part always makes me want to cry," Millie told him. "It's so beautiful."

"What a woman. You get it from her. God, every bit of it."

"Every bit of what?"

"Your fightin' spirit. Your strength. Your loyalty. Straight from Melisande to Melisande."

Millie touched the diary's pages reverently. "I admire her so much. She was the kind of woman who inspires men."

"And I'd say you're the same."

Millie's heart skipped a beat as she gazed up into Brig's solemn eyes. "No," she murmured. "I terrorize men."

"Do I look scared?"

"Not yet." She lowered her eyes and stared moodily at the diary.

Brig grimaced. He knew arguing would do no good. Nor would any of his heartfelt words. She knew that he loved her, but she would always hold part of her trust back, afraid that he loved her in spite of her unconventional nature, rather than because of it. He would have to convince her of the truth slowly and subtly.

Brig got up, stretched, then strolled to the far side of the sturdy oak coffee table by the couch. He sat down cross-legged, facing her, and put his elbow squarely in the center of the table. "Enough of this romantical history. Let's arm wrestle."

She looked at him in amazement. No man other than her brothers had ever asked her to arm wrestle. She liked the idea. She slapped her elbow onto the table and smiled wickedly. "You have to take a handicap, of course. Otherwise I won't have a fair chance. I'm the first to admit that you've got more muscles than I do." Her eyes twinkled. "Over the past few days, I've noticed little differences like that."

"Let's see. I'm nearly a foot taller than you and seventy pounds heavier. But then, you've got sharp fingernails, and you wear perfume, which is likely to distract me. Nope. We're an even match."

"Bullfeathers. How about I use both hands?"

"Aw, all right, you little sissy."

She anchored both hands to his. Their eyes met, sturdy blues teasing determined greens. "You say go," he told her.

"Give me a second to adjust my grip. . . . Go!"

"Cheat!"

She levered all one-hundred-and-five pounds into her sneak attack, and the veins stood out in his forearm as he struggled to keep her from thumping his hand down. She didn't play coy, straining prettily with no intention of trying to beat him. She tried like hell.

He slowly got his hand back to center, but by now she was half-lying, half-crouched on the floor, her bare heels sliding on its cool, flat tiles as she shoved against his superior strength. The well-honed muscles in her thighs showed below her white shorts, and her breasts strained wantonly under the white T-shirt she wore without a bra.

Brig felt distracted, but he tried to keep up appearances. "How you doin', little girl?" he taunted.

"Eat my dust, you cheeky dill."

"Never shoulda taught you how to talk Aussie."

She was soon sleek and glistening with perspiration. Her breath came in tiny pants. Her fingers grasped at his hand rhythmically. Her nipples were dark, upthrust imprints on the T-shirt.

Brig groaned. She didn't fight fair.

He felt the blood pounding low in his groin and wondered how he had enough concentration left to put up a show of winning. Hell, he wasn't winning, he was just holding his own. Of course, he wasn't trying too hard. The view was distracting, but worth preserving.

But he had to give the battle his best effort, because if he let her win, she'd sense his fakery. Caught between Millie's pride and a hard place, he thought wryly. A *very* hard place.

"Let's call a draw," he ordered between gritted teeth.

"Quitter!"

"Don't want to break your spirit."

"Don't want to admit defeat," she countered.

Shock tactics. They were his best choice. "Don't want to go off, and I will if I don't stop starin' at your fan-tas-tic norks."

Millie understood enough Australian slang to know that she'd just received a glorious, if somewhat earthy, compliment. Her mouth gaped and her grip faltered. *Whump.* He won easily, before she even noticed.

Gulping for air, she withdrew her hands. A proud glow came into her eyes. "You think I'm sexy when I arm wrestle?" she asked in amazement.

He was breathing hard himself, so he simply nodded. Even though one corner of his mouth teased her, the desire in his eyes was utterly sincere.

Millie stood up, poised on the balls of her feet. His gaze became predatory. His eyes never left hers as he slowly rose to a crouching position, his hands flat on the coffee table. She watched the muscles tightening in his powerful torso. Her heart thudded in anticipation.

Millie spun around and raced for the kitchen. She heard the lithe padding of his bare feet as he leaped after her. She heard a living room chair scrape back harshly as he shoved it out of his way. She opened the door to the back porch, and he was right behind her.

She nearly knocked the outer door off its hinges in her hurry to leave the porch. Millie ignored the steps and bounded gracefully to the grassy earth. She flung her arms high with victory. Brig grabbed her around the waist, and they went down on the soft ground in a heap.

It was all over in a matter of seconds. Their clothes lay scattered within throwing distance of their naked bodies. The white light of a huge summer moon cascaded over them, casting erotic shadows on the contrast between male and female. The night animals ceased speaking in the forest around them, enthralled, perhaps, by the low, intriguing sounds of laughter and passion.

Humming. He was humming against her stomach. Millie woke up as the husky vibrato in Brig's throat sizzled through her belly, warming her. She was smiling as she opened her eyes to the morning sunlight that streamed across the bed. A breeze from the open window flickered over her bare skin, and she realized without looking that the only thing covering her body was Brig. He had both arms around her hips.

With a sigh of delight, Millie lifted a hand and wound her fingers into his hair. Their life together would be perfect if it could just stay like this. "G'morning, love," she whispered.

His voice rumbled against her navel. "Since it's your day off, I figured I'd sing you awake slow."

"How about a duet?"

He chuckled. "Aw, me little Melisande, you're as pretty as a canary, but you sing like a buzzard."

When she laughed, he pressed his mouth to a tender spot several inches below her navel. Millie stopped laughing and made a soft whimpering sound. "I had a different kind of duet in mind," she murmured.

"Now *that* sounds promisin'."

He moved upwards slowly, kissing as he went. As he settled his body between her legs, she smiled at his half-shut eyes and sleep-rumpled face. "There is nothing sexier than the way you look in the morning, sir."

Brig winked. "You should see yourself." His eyes roamed over her greedily. "About this duet . . ."

"I can't sing, but I have other talents."

He stroked one of her breasts. "Show me what that mouth of yours is good for then." Millie cupped his face between her hands and drew him to her for a long, intimate kiss. "Oh, I like this kind of talent."

Millie arched against him, seeking the hardness that kept nudging her. "Let's start the concert."

Some time later, when the concert had ended, she ventured the opinion that their duet rated a standing ovation. He dutifully got out of bed and applauded. Then he bowed to her return applause and lay down again.

Millie pulled a sheet over him as he burrowed into a pillow and yawned lazily. "After a performance like yours, you deserve a nap," she said. "I'll fix breakfast."

"Grand idea, love."

"I thought you'd think so."

Millie put on a faded print sundress that flopped loosely around her body. Barefoot, she went into the kitchen and started a pot of water, then walked outside to pick flowers from a bed at the edge of the yard.

A battered blue van pulled into the driveway and stopped. Millie left her flowers in a pile and straightened warily, eyeing the unfamiliar vehicle. Two scruffy-looking men got out and ambled toward her.

Millie bent quickly and scooped up several hard clods of dirt. "Get off my property," she hissed.

One of the men laughed. "We want breakfast," he told her in a commanding tone.

"Bacon and eggs, toast, grits," his companion instructed.

"Get your own bacon. Go kiss a pig." Millie drew back her right arm and began throwing dirt clods with a speed and strength honed in years of playing baseball with two brothers. She caught one of the men in the chest, the other on the side of the head. They cursed loudly and ran toward her with the powerful strides of natural athletes.

Screeching like a banshee, Millie swung around and raced for the backdoor. What she lacked in size she made up for in speed. She passed her bedroom window a dozen feet ahead of the men.

They never got passed the window.

Millie heard the harsh sounds of two bodies colliding and hitting the ground. She whirled around and stared as Brig, in a pair of cutoffs, rolled off the stomach of one downed pursuer. He had a pistol in his hand, and he leveled it at the other man, who simply stopped and gazed at him with fascination.

"Budge an inch and you'll need a doctor," Brig told him in a calm, lethal tone.

The man on the ground held his pummeled stomach and squinted from Brig to Millie. In a cold, deep voice he demanded, "Who the hell is this bastard, Millie?"

Brig gave the men a look that was half-frown and half-bewilderment. "Who the hell are you bastards?" he growled.

Millie clasped both hands to her mouth to keep from laughing. "My brothers."

Eight

It was amazing that three men could be so different and yet agree so much on one thing—that she should fix breakfast while they lolled around her kitchen table recovering from their introduction.

Ordinarily Millie would have rebelled and demanded help, but this time she didn't want to disturb the cautious interplay between Brig and her brothers. Jeopard and Kyle had long ago acknowledged that she was a normal, mature woman entitled to male companionship, but they had never seen living proof before.

They propped their chins on their hands and questioned Brig with smooth, deceptive politeness. Kyle, a country music fan, was somewhat mollified. Jeopard, who avoided music and other gentle things as if they could hurt him, had no idea who Brig McKay was, other than being the man who had tackled him from his sister's bedroom window.

Brig kept a half-smile on his face and gave as good as he got. Millie's chest swelled with pride, and she could tell that Jeopard and Kyle were grudgingly impressed.

As she scrambled eggs, she affectionately studied her brothers. Neither was more than six feet tall, but they had an almost palpable air of confidence that made them seem much larger. Kyle's hair was nearly the same sunshine blond as hers, but Jeopard's was much darker.

Both men had inherited their father's clean, strong features, but women never described Kyle as handsome. The lack of conventional good looks had never stopped him from successfully romancing half the women in the known world, however.

Jeopard, on the other hand, had the kind of spellbinding handsomeness that belonged on a movie screen, though people took one look at the reserved, almost angry glitter in his eyes and never suggested that to him personally. Millie chewed her lower lip and frowned anxiously at her older brother. She worried about both him and Kyle, because their undercover work for navy intelligence had taken its toll over the years. But at least Kyle could still laugh. Jeopard had lost that ability.

She knew they'd seen death up close on more than one occasion. She suspected, though they'd never told her directly, that they'd killed men in the course of their work. They'd both been wounded; they'd both lost friends; worst of all, Jeopard had lost a lover, a civilian with whom he became involved during a mysterious mission in Europe.

Sometimes they worked as a team, but just as often they went separate ways to the far corners of the world. Their work was highly classified, so she rarely knew where they were or when they might come back. She didn't know why they were in Florida now, or what undercover work dictated that they wear grubby, faded jeans and old work shirts.

She *did* know, however, that they were treading on thin ice as far as her personal life was concerned.

"So, you'll go back to Nashville soon," Jeopard stated flatly, his mouth a grim line as he waited for Brig's response.

The picture of calm, Brig leaned back in his chair and sipped a cup of tea. "Yep." He scrutinized Jeopard silently, his eyes narrowed.

Millie watched her brother's expression register respect. Few men responded to Jeopard's authority with such nonchalance.

"Been puttin' it off," Brig added. "Can't wait much longer."

"And what about my sister?"

Millie smacked a spatula onto the stove top. "Your sister will be thirty years old this fall. She looks after herself."

"We know that, Millie," Kyle said. "But we also know that you take relationships seriously."

She slapped eggs and bacon onto a platter with quick, angry little motions. "I should imitate my big brothers and play the field."

"Melisande, don't get riled," Brig urged softly.

"*Melisande*?" Jeopard repeated.

Millie glanced up and saw his mouth twitch as he tried to suppress a smile. She raised her chin proudly and told both him and Kyle, "I've started using my full name sometimes. If you don't want to wear your breakfast for a hat, you'll pick another subject."

"Good girl," Brig commented. Then he set his mug down, leaned forward, and looked from Kyle to Jeopard slowly. His eyes were intensely serious. "I'm gonna marry your sister."

Millie dropped her spatula on the floor. After a stunned moment, she said firmly, "No, you're not."

He acknowledged her protest with a lazy wave of one hand. His gaze still on Jeopard and Kyle, he added, "She just hasn't said yes yet."

"I haven't been asked yet!"

He glanced at her. "But you figured on it, didn't you?"

Millie picked up the spatula and threatened him with it. He sighed and looked at her in mild exasperation.

"Melly, I know it's gonna be a while before you quit worryin' that you're not right for me, but after you relax, we'll get married. I'll do the real proposin' when the time comes."

Kyle and Jeopard shared a look. Kyle began to laugh, and even Jeopard managed a smile. Millie swung the spatula toward them. "It's not funny!"

Jeopard frowned at her. "If you take a man to bed, you ought to at least consider marrying him."

"*Damn*, Jep, don't you dare lecture me!"

"Why wouldn't you be right for him? What are you worrying about?"

She threw the spatula in the sink with a force that sent it bouncing out again. "I'm not very domestic!"

"Well, we can certainly see that," Kyle noted dryly.

"You guys and Dad made me this way! I don't fit in with traditional female behavior. I don't even *want* to fit in, and Brig thinks we'll be fine despite that!"

Brig stood up, his eyes troubled. He came over to the stove and got a plate full of toast. "Which is for you and me to discuss alone. Bring the rest of the food over and let's eat."

"Our future can't be reduced to the level of scrambled eggs."

"Our future doesn't have to be decided in front of your brothers."

"Eat without me. I'll be in my bedroom." Millie started toward the door.

"You walk out, I'm comin' after you."

"Bring my brothers. You'll need help."

She left the room. Brig looked down at Kyle and Jeopard. After a moment, Jeopard said, "You have our blessings, pal. You're a helluva fighter, but I think you've met your match."

Brig nodded and sat down. "What the devil did you blokes teach her when she was a kid?"

Kyle cursed softly. "Not us. The old man. Dad used to tell her that women only need men for one thing—protection. Financial, emotional, and physical protection. He didn't want her to need anyone that way."

Jeopard agreed. "The old man was bitter toward women. It has to do with the fact that our mother planned to divorce him after Millie was born."

Brig whistled under his breath. This was a story he'd never heard. "But she died," he noted. "Didn't it have something to do with Melisande's birth?"

"Not really," Jeopard answered. "I was only seven when it happened, but I remember that Mother was always frail. She caught pneumonia a few months after

Millie was born." He paused. "She couldn't take mili
tary life, and the old man never forgave her for being s
weak. I think it just tore him up that she didn't lov
him enough to keep trying."

Kyle added, "So he made sure there'd be nothing
weak about Millie. Jep and I didn't know any better—w
were just kids ourselves. Dad treated Millie like a son
so we treated Millie like a brother."

"Well, I've gotta find a way to convince your *brother*
that I like her just the way she is," Brig said flatly.

Kyle arched a brow. "You'll have to let her protec
you then. And you better learn to like it—or *fak*
liking it."

Brig chuckled ruefully. "I should let her wrestle a
mugger while I just watch?"

"Something like that," Jeopard admitted.

"That's what ruined her romance with that guy i
Birmingham," Kyle reminded his brother.

"Good. Political geek."

"Amen," Brig added. "I *like* Melly's spirit. He didn't.
He paused, thinking. "But she's so damned little. Sh
takes too many risks. I've seen her do things sh
oughtn't do, and I couldn't resist helpin' her out. Ever
so, I'm damned proud of her. And she's startin' t
believe me when I tell her so."

"She'll believe you until the day she does somethin
that scares you so much that you forget to be proud o
her," Kyle warned. "Remember that."

Brig eyed him thoughtfully. "Good advice," he ad
mitted.

Kyle stuck out a hand. "Good luck." They shook.

Brig held out his hand to Jeopard. For a moment, h
and Millie's older brother traded assessing looks, meas
uring each other's strengths. Brig thought there was
good man behind those cold eyes. Jeopard proved it b
grasping his outstretched hand and shaking firmly.

"She loves you," Jeopard told him. "It was obvious b
the look on her face when she introduced us."

"I love her. You can count on it."

With that understanding established, they sat bacl

and looked at the empty chair at the table. Brig got up silently and left the room. When he came back, he carried Millie under one arm. She dangled there rigidly, half-mad and half-amused.

He put her down by her chair, and she glared at him. "If I weren't hungry, I would never have let you do that," she promised.

"Hah."

She sat down while he went to the stove and got the rest of the food. Millie looked at her brothers, who gazed back with feigned innocence. "Don't say a word," she ordered.

Jeopard and Kyle climbed back in their old van and left after lunch. Brig stood beside her at the edge of the yard as she waved good-bye.

When the van was out of sight beyond her moss-draped oak trees, Millie leaned against him, her arms crossed tightly over her stomach. He slipped an arm around her shoulders.

"Sssh, now, sssh," he urged. "They're Surprises, remember? I'd bet my next record contract that they can take care of themselves and anybody else that comes along."

She looked up at him in amazement. "How do you do it?" Millie demanded.

"Do what, love?"

"Read my mind."

He chuckled. "It's an old aborigine trick."

She stood on tiptoe and kissed him gently. "Thank you for caring, you old aborigine." He hugged her, and she sighed into the warm texture of the blue polo shirt he now wore with his cutoffs. "When are you going back to Nashville?" she asked in a carefully neutral tone.

"When you agree to come with me."

She stiffened and drew back to look up at him with luminous, unhappy eyes. "You can't wait that long. I know you've been asked to play at a charity concert next weekend. I know that your manager wants you to come back tomorrow."

He frowned. "You readin' minds too?"

"I called your manager and grilled him about your schedule."

"Strewth! I'll twist Chuck's tongue around his neck!"

"He simply told me the truth. Don't be mad at him."

Brig grabbed her hands. "Melisande, what would you leave behind if you came with me? Nothing. Just this old place. Just a job with the sheriff's department, a job somebody else can do. I know you love your home, and I'll hire somebody to take care of it. I'll donate money to the city if it'll keep you from feelin' guilty about leavin' your job without two weeks notice."

"Those aren't the important problems."

"I've got a helluva big house outside Nashville. Country-style. Quiet. Plenty of room for even the most rambunctious woman. You can have the run of it—"

"And play pampered mistress while you work?"

"Come to work with me. I'll find something for you to do."

She laughed tonelessly. "I guess I could learn to be a groupie or a gopher."

An impressive mixture of Australian and American obscenities rolled off his tongue. "What do you *want* to do, then?"

Millie held his hands tightly. She wanted to go with him and never look back, but she was afraid. "I'll visit you," she murmured. "On my days off. During vacations. And we'll see how well I fit into your life."

A muscle worked in his jaw. "My life is you."

"Your life is me and your music. You try to sound casual about it, but I'd have to be a fool not to see how much it means to you. Anyone who hurts your music, hurts you." She struggled with the tightness in her throat. "I don't want to be that anyone."

"What do you think you'd do that could hurt my music or me?"

"I know what kind of fans you attract. They're rowdy and unpredictable. Fights are practically a part of your show. I couldn't stand by and watch like a good little girl."

"Those were the old days," he said in an amazed tone. "Last tour me and the band went on, we didn't get into more than one or two fights the whole time. I don't play backwoods bars anymore."

"You admitted to me once that women throw themselves at you back stage. I'm afraid I'd throw them back—with their noses rearranged."

He tried to joke. "You've got my permission."

"The law suits wouldn't be funny, and you know it."

All Brig could picture was a backstage without her waiting for him. "Melly, you're not giving it a chance," he said angrily. "You don't know how you'd act."

She nodded. "And that's why I'll come for short visits, and we'll see."

He stepped back from her, so frustrated that all he could do was shake his head. "Some sort of mean angel made me fall in love with you," he told her solemnly. "And now I'm ruined for any other woman." He shook a finger at her. "But if I'd had a choice—"

The soft purr of a powerful car engine made them both look toward the bend in her driveway. A long black limousine pulled into sight. "If your brothers are comin' back, they changed their cover in a big way," Brig commented. The limo stopped beside them.

A driver got out, nodded a greeting, and opened the backdoor. The occupant put both feet on the ground, and Millie noted with a sinking sensation that neither Jeopard nor Kyle Surprise had feminine legs. And they sure didn't wear white hose or blue pumps with small blue rosettes on the toes.

"Honey, I flew down from Nashville because I just can't go on alone anymore!" a sugary voice blurted.

Natty Brannigan followed her legs out of the limousine, dabbed white gloves at the tears on her perfect face, and flung herself into Brig's arms.

If he'd had a choice.

• • •

"And then this huge, shadowy man stepped out of the hallway at the studio, and he grabbed me around the throat," Natty continued. Seated on Millie's couch, a cup of blackberry tea perched on the gray silk skirt that matched her gray silk jacket and blouse, Natty held court. Millie sat cross-legged in a chair and aimed black thoughts in Natty's direction. Brig sat beside Natty on the couch, his arm around her.

"It was late at night—I don't know how he got past the security people," Natty continued. "But he held my throat so tight that I could barely breathe, and he said, 'You like to sing, don't you?' I was about to faint, but I nodded. 'Then stick to singing and stay out of other people's business,' he said. And then he let go of me. I blacked out for a second, and when I came to, I was sitting on the floor, and he was gone."

"And nobody else got a look at him?" Brig asked.

She shook her head. "Oh, Brig." She moaned. "After the incident with the car brakes and the vandalism at my house, it all adds up. Don't you see? He's trying to scare me off!"

Millie's dark thoughts gave way to curiosity. Natty looked at her suddenly and asked, "Has Brig told you about me?"

The dark thoughts returned. Millie shook her head. "I didn't ask for a list of ex-girlfriends." In truth, she'd figured that what she didn't know couldn't hurt her.

"Mercy!" Natty exclaimed. "Brig honey, is that what she still thinks I am?"

"She's not an ex-girlfriend," Brig told Millie patiently. He removed his arm from Natty's shoulders, patted her hand, and looked at Millie with droll rebuke. "If you want a list, I'll give you one. But Natty's not on it. If you had the typical curiosity God gave a female, you'd have asked by now, and I'd have told you so. I kept expectin you to."

He and Millie shared a long look. Relief bubbled up inside her as she read the unmistakable truth in Brig's eyes. She gave him an embarrassed squint and mumbled, "Sexist goat. I apologize for not being nosy."

Brig nodded. "Want to know the whole tale?" Her head bobbed up and down enthusiastically. "That Tennessee senator I punched, Natty was seeing him."

"Let's be accurate," Natty interjected wearily. "I was havin' a torrid affair with the man." She sighed. "Bo Halford is one handsome devil, I admit it. With the emphasis on *devil*."

"Natty found out that Bo was lettin' chemical companies set up toxic waste dumps without goin' through the state environmental protection boys," Brig explained. "Takin' payoffs for it."

"He was putting these awful ol' dumps outside little mountain towns that I love," Natty said emphatically. "I have relatives up thataway. I had to do somethin'."

"So she decided to blow the whistle on Bo," Brig added.

Natty inhaled sadly. "And I was afraid of what he'd do—his family's been in Tennessee politics since before the Civil War. You don't mess with a man like Bo Halford. So Brig said he'd go with me when I put my cards on the table."

"How did you end up hitting him?" Millie asked Brig, her tone incredulous.

"He told Natty that she'd never get enough evidence to hurt him, and he'd hurt *her* plenty if she tried."

Natty gestured excitedly. "And that's when ol' Brig popped him. Right in the nose! Bo took a swing back, and Brig punched him in the breadbasket. Bo went down like a felled tree! It was beautiful!"

Millie stared at Natty Brannigan with growing admiration. Under that debutante exterior lurked a tiger's heart.

The singer looked at Brig sadly. "But Brig ended up in jail, despite everything his people and my people could do." She pressed a hand to her chest. "I still shudder when I think of what would have happened if we hadn't got you transferred to the jail down here."

"What?" Millie asked, amazed. She gazed at Brig wide-eyed. "I thought your lawyers arranged the transfer to avoid bad publicity."

"Bad publicity and accidents." He shrugged.

"Accidents caused by Bo Halford's people in a Nashville jail," Natty explained grimly. "Somebody would have probably killed him." She teared up again. "Somebody still might try. I think Bo's tryin' to warn me, and Lord knows what he'd do to you if you go back to Nashville before the federal people get done."

Millie's train of thought had stopped at the words, "Somebody still might try." Trembling, she stood up. "You're in danger," she told Brig. "I'm definitely going to Nashville with you."

He groaned. "I don't know if I'm in danger. I might not be." He rose and went to her, grasping her shoulders tightly. "But since I'm not sure anymore, the last thing I'm gonna do is put you in the middle. You'll stay here."

"No."

"Yep, Melly. For the time bein'."

"What are you going to do?" she asked desperately. "Wait for the man to try something?"

"That's all I can do until the investigation's done."

"What investigation?"

"Federal boys are workin' on the case. That's why Bo's harassin' Natty. He's startin' to squirm."

"Then you stay here. There's nothing you can do."

Brig's jaw tightened. "I've got business to take care of. And I'm not used to hidin' like a scared rabbit. Besides, it's not likely that the mangy bastard'll try anything serious."

Millie touched her chest tentatively. Her heart was trying to pound a dent in her ribcage. She felt cold and terrified in a strange way she'd never experienced before.

"Melisande?" Brig asked with concern.

She gazed at him wretchedly. "I'm frightened for your sake."

His eyes melted with tenderness. He took her in his arms and swayed gently, holding her. "You stay here and don't worry," he whispered. After a moment he said, "And I think Natty ought to stay with you. It's a good, safe place for her to be. There now. You can protect Natty."

"I *love* being protected," Natty added quickly. "If you don't mind the company."

Millie drew back and looked at Brig with desperate adoration. "I don't know if I can let you go and not follow," she murmured.

"A little while ago you were ready to let me go alone," he reminded her gently.

"I didn't think you were in danger then."

"No more worries that you'll embarrass me?"

She shook her head fervently. "I don't care about anything but keeping you alive."

He made a soft sound of bittersweet joy and kissed her forehead. "Bo Halford's not in a killin' mood. He just wants to have some fun, Melly."

"Then why can't I go with you?"

Brig's eyes darkened with exasperation. "If he hurt you, I'd mangle him. And then I'd spend the rest of my life in a jail. One not half so kindly as Paradise Springs, eh?"

Millie grasped his shirt front. Her anxiety quieted suddenly, replaced by absolute, deadly calm. "If anything happens to you, Halford won't get away from me."

The silence that followed was charged with emotion. The only sound was the soft catch of Natty's breath as she watched Brig and Millie. "God," she prayed out loud in utter sincerity, "Please let me find somebody to love that much."

Nine

Brig realized how much he missed Millie after only a few days back in Nashville. He was holding Rucker and Dinah McClure hostage just to hear them talk about her. Rucker barely stifled a yawn over his bourbon.

"I hate to mention this, but it's getting late," Dinah interrupted gently. She glanced around the swank Nashville restaurant to which Brig had invited them as soon as he heard that Rucker was in town on a book promotion tour. "It's just us and the waiters. And the waiters are forming a vigilante committee to kick us out."

"Come on out to my house," Brig urged.

Rucker rubbed a hand across his thick auburn mustache and chuckled. "Friend, I've told you every true story I know about Millie, and a few I made up."

Brig groaned and leaned back in his chair. He felt awkward in his black sport coat, tan slacks, crisp shirt, and tie. It wasn't that he didn't like dressing up on occasion—it was just that he wanted to be back in the Florida heat, wearing little or nothing, with Millie.

"It's not fair," he grumbled lightly. "I've written dozens of songs about the hell of bein' lonely. Nobody warned me that they were true."

"Takes a special love to make the loneliness hurt so bad," Rucker noted.

Brig watched as he reached over and squeezed his wife's hand. She gave her husband a look that said he was going to get extra-special treatment back in their hotel room tonight. Brig succumbed to an ache of pure envy.

"Did you know that Millie likes children?" Dinah offered. "She says they're the only people smaller than she is."

Brig nodded. "We're gonna have about a dozen."

Rucker propped his chin on one hand. "I don't think she likes them *that* much."

"I'll compromise. Maybe have two or three of our own, then adopt a bunch."

"Good plan," Dinah noted wryly.

"I can imagine Melisande holdin' our baby," Brig said hoarsely. He raised one big hand as if he were touching someone visible only to him. Dropping the hand atop his bourbon glass, he brought it to his mouth and downed the contents in one swallow. "Lord, I've turned sentimental. Sorry."

"I think Millie's very lucky," Dinah told him, smiling.

"Why don't you bring her to Birmingham next weekend?" Rucker asked. "When you do that big charity concert. Your troubles with the state senator wouldn't stretch to another state, would they?"

"Maybe not." Brig thought for a minute, gauging the safety factors. "I could hire a couple of security people to stick with Melisande the whole time. Maybe. Yeah." Revitalized, he grinned. "I set you two free. You've cheered me up."

The three of them left the restaurant and stood amid the glitter of downtown, waiting for a cab. Brig glanced sideways as two hulking men in denim and tractor caps stepped from the shadows of a nearby building. He could tell that they were headed straight for him. Autograph seekers, most likely, but with an air of menace that caused his body to tighten in defense.

"Thought it was him," one man said to the other.

"Yeah, it's him."

"Hello, mates," Brig said, as they swaggered to a stop less than an arm's length away. "I'm him."

"We just want to tell you that you are one ugly son of a—"

"I got a lady here," Rucker interrupted, his tone low and lethal.

They leered at Dinah. "How much does a classy one like her cost?"

"Oh, wonderful," Dinah murmured in mild disgust. She grabbed Rucker's arm as he stepped in front of her, his fists clenched. "You can't sign books with your knuckles bandaged."

Brig angled in front of them both. He felt the cool flow of adrenaline into his muscles. It was always like this before a fight. "You blokes got business with me, not with my friends. Say what you got to say."

His neutral remark provoked a long stream of obscenities from one man, while the other grinned. Brig waited with a patient look on his face, while he calculated which man would be easier to slug first.

"You boys aren't happy," he told them succinctly.

"What you gonna do about it?"

"Before I kick your butts, maybe you could let me in on the reason. Man wants to fight me, he's usually got good cause."

"We don't need no cause."

A small alarm went off in Brig's mind. He smiled, while recognition gnawed at his stomach. "You boys wouldn't be workin' for Senator Halford, would you? 'Cause he knows I have to be on me best behavior until I get off parole. I just remembered that I could go back to jail if I was to lose me temper."

"Don't know no Senator Halford," one man said too quickly. Brig's eyes caught the flicker of caution in his face.

"If you want to fight me, you'll have to do it without my help." Brig held up both hands. "Go ahead. My friends here'll tell the police exactly what happened."

"Aw, to hell with you. You're crazy."

The men turned and left quickly. Brig watched them

until they disappeared around a corner. "Crazy like a fox," he muttered. He turned around to find Rucker and Dinah gazing at. him in concern. "No worries, folks." But his voice was grim. "Let's not mention this to Melisande, eh?"

"Are you still going to bring her to Birmingham?" Dinah asked.

"No way." The night turned ten shades darker, and loneliness closed in on him again.

Millie pulled the reclining chair upright with a decisive movement. "I'm going to that concert in Birmingham," she announced flatly.

From her place on the couch, where she was painting her toenails a muted burgundy color, Natty's hand jerked, and she smeared burgundy across her instep. "You are not."

"Raybo knows you're here. He'll send Suds or Charlie over to check on you."

"I'm not worried about *me*, honey."

"I'll be fine. The problems are in Tennessee, not Alabama."

"Ever hear of little ol' cars, trains, and airplanes?" Natty drawled. "Problems can travel."

Millie got up and paced. "I can't stand it. Brig's so damned cheerful on the telephone. Something's wrong!"

"It won't be made right by you sashayin' off to see him. He'll be upset."

"At first he'll be upset. Then he'll relax."

"Mercy, girl, you don't give up."

"Will you help me? This concert—it's a formal thing. He's going to wear some sort of tuxedo. What should I take to wear?"

"An armored body suit."

"Be serious, Natty!"

"You're determined?"

"I'm determined."

Natty sighed. Then she picked up a phone on the coffee table and punched so many buttons that Millie knew the call was long distance. "Tito, honey, this is Natty. Sorry to call you at home, but I need an itsy bitsy favor. Can you ship some dresses to me tomorrow? Hmmm, just a loan. Lord, yes, I'll mention your name on my cable show next month. Send cocktail type and everyday stuff too. Sexy but not indecent, honey. Street length. No, they're for a friend." Natty cupped her hand over the phone. "What size are you?"

"Four petite."

"I hate your little ol' doll-sized guts." Natty put the phone to her mouth again. "Tito, four petite. And send accessories, honey."

"I need purses big enough to hold a handgun."

"Tito, this is for a Little Miss Rambo. Make sure she can pack a pistol in the purses. Hmmm? Honey, don't. Don't get hysterical. I know Italian designers get hysterical easy, but you calm down. I'll explain later."

Millie listened with quiet fascination. Natty gave the hysterical Tito her address, soothed his nerves for a few minutes, and hung up.

"Thanks, Nat. I owe you one."

"Honey, I just want you to be happy. When Brig sees you in one of Tito's dresses, he'll be so dazzled he'll temporarily forget to paddle your fanny."

Brig spent all morning and most of the afternoon rehearsing with his band. Since the concert wasn't until Saturday, he now had a long Friday night ahead of him in a luxurious but lonely hotel room. The only bright spot was the phone call he planned to make to Florida, just as soon as he took a bath. He ordered a sandwich from room service, unlocked the door, and ran a tub full of steaming water.

Twenty minutes later he heard someone knocking. "Bring it in and leave it on the bed!" he yelled. Brig dumped shampoo on his hair and shut his eyes.

His head was covered in lather by the time he heard, "I'll put it on the bed if you like, but I'd rather put it in the tub."

The voice. Low, husky, female, with more than a hint of the south. Brig slung soap from his face. "*Melisande.*" She stood in the bathroom door, smiling tentatively while her eyes roamed over him with desperate pleasure. "What are you doin' here?" he demanded gruffly. Then, in amazement, "Strewth!"

He'd finally noticed that she looked different. Millie proudly glanced down at the swirling silk dress she wore. The green color matched her eyes. Delicate appliqués rimmed the discreet, but plunging, neckline. She felt willowly in high-heeled shoes. She touched her hair. The blond curls usually did what they pleased, but today she'd tamed them into sleek waves. And Natty had loaned her some light makeup.

"I had to see you," she told him bluntly. "If you send me away—"

"You have to go back to Florida, dammit." He exhaled, as if getting himself under control. "Stubborn Tasmanian devil. Reckless little she-wolf."

"How do I look?"

His voice rose. "Good enough to eat! Now go call the airport and book yourself on a flight back!"

"No." She took two steps toward him. "I love you, and I want to be with you. Even if it's just for a couple of days. Birmingham is safe, Brig. Please."

"I told you to stay in Florida!"

"Why are you yelling?" She took another step toward him, her body aching for his touch. "I'll take anything you can give me. A few minutes. An hour. One night." Her voice trembled. "I know you just left Florida a few days ago, but I miss you." She fought for control. "I worry about you. I came here even though I knew you'd be furious. That's one reason I wanted to look pretty. To distract you."

"Melisande," he said, half-groaning her name. "Stop it. It's not fair for you to dress up. I'd have trouble resistin' if you wore a burlap bag and army boots."

"I know. I have feminine wiles."

"Feminine *wilds.*"

She held out her hands and stepped closer. "I love you," she whispered.

"That does it," he said in a low growl of a voice. He grabbed her hand and pulled. Millie sank down on the side of the tub and yelped with delight as his wet arms went around her. She wasn't certain whether he dragged her into the tub with him or whether she climbed in. The end result was the same. She lay on top of him, kissing him wantonly, her legs entwined with his. The skirt of her dress floated like a green cloud.

"Tito is going to get hysterical over this," she murmured breathlessly.

"Who? Kiss my neck."

Someone knocked on the door.

"Bring it in and put it on the bed!" Brig yelled, his voice strained.

The room service waiter breezed past the open bathroom door, glanced in, and nearly dropped his tray. Millie looked over her shoulder at the young man's startled expression.

"G'day, mate," Brig said cheerfully. "You've heard about my reputation with the ladies, eh?"

"Hi. I'll . . . I'll come back later with the check."

"Sign it for me, eh? And throw in about thirty percent for yourself."

"Thank you, Mr. McKay!"

"And lock the door behind you."

"Yes, sir!"

After the waiter left, Millie burst into soft laughter. "I think he blushed more than I did."

"Sheilas should blush. It's sexy."

Brig anchored his hands in her soggy skirt and eased both it and her slip up to her waist. His fingers scooted over her black panties and garter belt. "A full attack, I see. Nothin' left to chance."

"I'm devious. I can catch more flies with honey than with vinegar, Natty says."

"You're takin' your honey back home tonight."

"All right. I'll go quietly." Her eyes impish, she tried to push herself out of his arms.

"Later."

Millie slipped one hand deep into the water and stroked his thighs, taking liberal side trips to other, more private areas. "My, that's a mean crocodile."

"Lonesome." His hand sidled over her panties, then gripped them and tugged harshly. The filmy silk ripped apart, and he drew it away from her body.

"What soothes the savage beast?" she purred.

He closed his eyes and shuddered, all teasing lost. "Only you, Melly," he whispered. "Only you."

She caught a soft moan in her throat and kissed him. Straddling his body, she eased herself fully onto his hard flesh. The sensation was so sublime that she bowed her head next to his and whimpered his name. The water lapped at them and moved in sync with the slow rocking of her hips.

"Need me the way I need you," Brig murmured into her ear. "This way, and every way. Let me take care of you."

Millie lifted her head and gazed at him, her eyes full of pain. "You don't have to, Brig. I won't ever ask you for help. I'm not weak and dependent. Don't worry."

He recalled what her brothers had told him about their father's bitterness toward women. He tightened his arms around her. Somehow, patiently and with love, he would teach her that they could take care of each other.

"Are you tryin' to get me plastered, woman?"

"Yes." Curled beside him on the bed, her leg draped over his thighs, she tilted the champagne glass to his mouth once more.

He took a quick swallow. "Why?"

"So you'll go to sleep."

"And forget about sendin' you back to the airport."

"Right."

She raised her head from his shoulder and kissed the tip of his nose. Brig gazed up at her and sighed with a mixture of happiness and frustration. Her cheeks were still flushed from desire, and her lips were ruddy from kissing.

"The look you get after sex is just plain dangerous to my good sense," he protested mildly.

"Say I can stay with you this weekend then."

"*Strewth.*" He rolled away from her and sat on the edge of the bed, running his hands through his hair. She nestled against his back.

"I'll do whatever you want, if you'll let me stay."

He turned his head and studied her with shock. "Those are words I never thought I'd hear from you."

"I love you. I want to be with you. Nothing else matters. Look. Neither of us seriously believes that anything will happen."

He got up, went to the bathroom, and came back wearing a white terrycloth robe with the hotel's monogram. He carried a second robe in his hand. "Put this on. For my concentration's sake."

Smiling, she wrapped herself in the soft garment and tucked her legs under her. Millie watched him pace back and forth, his hands on his hips. Finally he halted and faced her. He pointed a finger in warning.

"There'll be no heroics from you," he ordered. "And I'll take the pistol you've got hidden somewhere."

She looked crestfallen. "You know me too well."

"Yep." He paused. "If I didn't think I was worryin' too much, I'd send you packing. As it is, I'm gonna get the biggest, meanest bodyguard in the state of Alabama to stay with you at the concert tomorrow night. Promise that you won't try to dodge him."

"I promise," she said solemnly.

"No heroics. Promise."

"I promise."

"On your honor, Melisande."

Her chin rose proudly. "On my honor. I won't give you a thing to worry about."

Brig knelt beside the bed and took her face between his hands. Concern for her washed away any trace of levity. His eyes were cold, his voice low and hard. "Don't cross me on this, Melisande."

She stared at him with a puzzled frown, amazed at the fierceness in his attitude. "I won't," she assured him gently.

When she reached out and caressed his jaw with one fingertip, his eyes flickered and the harshness left them. Millie tried to smile. She'd gratefully vow to ignore her protective instincts this once in order to please him, but a little knot of anxiety began to build under her breastbone. Would he expect her to make the vow permanent?

The next day they met his band backstage at the sprawling, modern Birmingham Civic Center, the site of the concert. The six men gathered around them, studying Millie curiously.

"Melisande Surprise," Brig told them.

"Howdy."

"Howdy."

"Howdy."

"Howdy."

"Stop," Brig complained jokingly. "Couldn't you boys do this in harmony?"

"Howdy," Millie told them. Her mouth crooked up in a wry smile. "That's a group howdy. You'll have to share it."

The blue-jeaned bunch grinned at her, and she could tell that their first impression was positive. It was mutual. They had clever eyes and well-lived-in faces. These men didn't believe in standing on the sidelines of life.

Two were Australian, musicians who'd been with Brig before he came to the States. Three were American. And one, who revealed short dreadlocks when he removed a battered western hat, was Jamaican.

He flashed a friendly smile at her and said in the lilting accent of his homeland, "I know what you're thinking. But though I'm black, I sing like a redneck."

Millie laughed. "Bravo. If an Aussie can sing at the Grand Ole Opry, so can you."

Each of the six had either a girlfriend or a wife to

introduce to her. The whole group finally made its way to a nearby steak restaurant and commandeered a small banquet room.

Joking insults flew back and forth between everyone at the table. Requests for ketchup and other condiments were handled bluntly, often with a deliciously rude comment thrown in for flavor.

"What kind of work do you do?" one of the girlfriends asked Millie.

"I'm a deputy sheriff."

She expected the politely stunned reaction that announcement usually received. Instead, everyone whooped and applauded.

"Brig's finally got the law on his side!"

"Justice is blind!"

"Aw, he ain't so ugly!"

"In the outback, he's considered a prize!"

"Yeah, but women there are desperate for any man who has a full set of teeth!"

Millie glanced at Brig's amused expression and knew that he was thoroughly comfortable at the center of such abuse. She loved his casual self-confidence.

"I wouldn't mind if he didn't have teeth," she said solemnly.

He clasped his chest in gratitude. "Thank you, love."

The bantering stopped as a giant man ambled into the room. Brig stood up and shook hands with him. Millie eyed the newcomer's pin-striped suit and knew it must be custom-made. No retailer sold suits that could fit a body the size of a small truck.

Brig turned toward her. "Melisande, I want you to meet Kitty O'Conner. The best bodyguard in the south."

She held out a hand. Kitty's hand swallowed it. She shook one of his fingers.

"Kitty, this is your client. Melisande Surprise."

"Hello," Kitty said in a soft, high-pitched voice. "You won't have a thing to worry about tonight."

Unless you accidentally step on me, Millie thought. "Kitty, I can believe it," she answered sincerely.

He nodded to Brig. "I'll meet you in the hotel lobby at seven."

As he left, she gazed after him in rapt curiosity. "Why is he called 'Kitty'?"

Brig was smiling thoughtfully as he sat down. "Don't know, love. Nobody's ever had the nerve to ask him."

"I not only feel protected, I feel overwhelmed. This is too much, Brig."

"You promised, Melisande."

She let her protest trail off as a warning glint came into his eyes. Something about it frightened her. She seriously doubted that Senator Halford would bother Brig here in Birmingham, and she knew that Brig doubted it too. Otherwise, he'd never have let her stay, bodyguard or no. But if Brig were this concerned for her safety, he must have reason to suspect the worse. He wasn't telling her everything.

Her appetite gone, she smiled numbly and listened to the group's banter begin again. They were wonderful people, and she sensed that they would accept her wholeheartedly. It was reassuring. Maybe Brig's world wasn't so different from her own.

But right now she was worried about tonight. With sudden, desperate certainty Millie knew that if anyone put Brig in danger, no promise would keep her from defending him.

Brig pounded playfully on the door. "Come out of the bathroom before I lose my patience!"

"Sounds as if you've already lost it!" Millie called.

"I've got something to show you!"

"I've got something to show *you*!"

She flung the door open, and they stared at each other. "*Strewth*," she said in soft awe, as she gazed at his black tux. It had a few western touches, and he wore a black string tie with the shirt, but the result was definitely elegant and definitely heart-stopping.

He chuckled at her pleased appraisal. "*Strewth* yourself," he returned, his eyes glowing. "Is that another of ol' Tito's outfits?"

"Yes." She glanced down at her blue dress. "Fancy, eh?"

"Does a kangaroo hop?" He took her in his arms. "I love it." He tilted his head to one side and peered at the glittering high-heeled shoes that matched her dress. "Perched on those you'll stay out of trouble. Can't chase anybody."

"Kitty can do the chasing," she told him. And she meant it. If at all possible, she wouldn't break her word to Brig.

Kitty, wearing a black tux that would have fit Bigfoot, was waiting for them downstairs. He nodded politely and stayed behind them as they went outside to the glossy white limo that waited. When autograph seekers stopped Brig by the door, Millie was subtly aware that Kitty stepped closer to her. She caught a glimpse of the shoulder pistol under his jacket.

"A six-shooter. Four-inch. Smith," she said, as he sat down across from them on the limo's jump seat. "One of my favorites."

His eyes widened. "Ma'am?"

"Your pistol. I have that model at home. Good weapon. A lot of kick though."

Kitty stared at her in silent awe. Brig slapped one thigh and laughed until tears edged his eyes. Wiping them away, he briefly told the bodyguard about her background. Kitty's polite demeanor held a new note of respect.

He trailed them like a shadow after they arrived at the civic center. Brig kept a hand on her arm and guided her through the chaos backstage. They stopped at a magnificent buffet and sipped wine.

"Do you know who that is?" she said with a gasp, as a tall, bearded man waved at him from the far end of the table. "That's Kenny Rogers!"

"I know, Melisande," Brig answered drolly. He waved back. "His dressin' room is next to mine."

"You should have told me!"

"I didn't know you were a fan of his."

"Of course! You saw all his records at my house!" She stopped, watching the amusement in Brig's blue eyes. "I like your music too," she said contritely.

Sighing, Brig took a cocktail fork from the table and held it pointed at his stomach. "You like Kenny better than me. My honor is ruined. Want to see my hors d'oeuvre impression?"

She laughed and whisked the fork away. "I only love one man in country music. And his name's not Kenny Rogers."

"Willie Nelson?"

"Brig McKay."

"Hmmm. Never heard of him." Grinning, he bent down and kissed her.

"He's the best," she whispered.

"Want to go to my dressing room now?"

"Is that an indecent proposition, sir?"

"Wish it were, but it's not. You'll see why ."

Arm in arm, with Kitty on their heels, they went down a flight of stairs to a maze of crowded halls. When they finally came to Brig's room, Millie found all six of his musicians lounging around.

"Ah. Communal," she observed.

"That's a polite description."

"Howdy," one of the guys said.

"Howdy," another added.

"Don't start that again, you mangy swamp rats," Brig commanded.

She sat in a corner chair and watched, intrigued, as they tuned instruments and warmed up. Kitty sat beside her, stoical and stone-faced. At ten o'clock, when the concert was half over, everyone went back upstairs.

Brig guided her to a spot where she could see from the wings. "Be back in about thirty minutes, love," he told her. His gaze went to Kitty, who nodded.

Millie shooed Brig away lightly. "Kitty and I will be just fine. Go sing, mate."

He kissed her and went to await his entrance with the band. What could happen now? Millie asked silently. Nothing. She was ready to enjoy the show. With a thrill of pride, she listened to the applause after the emcee introduced Brig and his group.

Halfway through the first song, she glanced at Kitty. Sweat was beaded on his face and his eyes were half-shut. Millie grabbed his arm. "Are you sick?"

"It's nothing serious, ma'am."

She tried to joke. "Of course it's serious! If you faint and fall on me, I'll be crushed."

"I think I'm coming down with the flu." He swayed a little.

Alarmed, Millie tugged on his arm. "Let's find you a place to sit. You can watch me from a short distance, can't you?"

"I suppose."

She spotted a chair at the top of the stairs to the dressing room area. Millie got him settled there. He tilted his head back and shut his eyes.

"I'll get you some aspirin from Brig's dressing room."

"I have to go with you."

"I'll be right back, for goodness sake!"

"Right back," he mumbled, and dabbed at his feverish face.

She went downstairs and ran into the dressing room. She stopped cold. She'd watched a security guard lock the door after everyone left the room.

Millie made a slow circle of the room, trying to determine if anything had been disturbed. She jumped at the sound of footsteps in the hall outside. The hall had been empty a moment ago. The steps halted by the door.

Acting on impulses honed by years of training, Millie moved fast. Just as the door opened, she dropped to all fours behind a couch. It was probably Kenny Rogers coming to visit, she told herself. What would she say? Hi, Kenny. I'm just checking for dust devils?

She peeked around the edge of the couch and watched a short, stocky man step into the room. He had the flattened features of a boxer and the big hands to match. She frowned. Handkerchiefs covered his fingers. He went to a long counter fronted by mirrors, reaching into his pockets as he moved.

Even from her awkward hiding place, Millie could see well enough to recognize the materials he spread out on the counter. He laid out small bags of white powder, several glass vials, and drug paraphernalia. Then he turned and hurriedly left the room, pulling the door shut behind him.

She leapt up, her hands clenched. It was such an obvious plant. Undoubtedly, boxer-face was heading for a telephone to place an anonymous call to the police. Boxer-face was probably working for Senator Halford.

And all she had to do was capture him.

Ten

She ran into the hallway in time to see him disappear around a corner. Millie chewed her lip in frustration. He was heading away from the stage area. Her promise to Brig held her frozen in place.

She started to scream for Kitty. No, the idea was too absurd. *Here Kitty, here Kitty.* And by the time the ailing bodyguard lumbered to her aid, the culprit would be gone.

If boxer-face worked for the senator, he was invaluable. Millie thought of what Halford might have done to Brig if he'd served time in a Tennessee jail. Brig might be maimed or dead. The senator could still make certain that he ended up that way. Defensive love erased her doubts.

"Forgive me for breaking my promise," she whispered raggedly, while kicking off her high heels to run after the intruder.

On stage, Brig was in the middle of his second song. He cradled an acoustic guitar in front of him and played it with a skilled abandon that brought cheers from the crowd. Feeling proud, he glanced toward the people in the wings, expecting to see Millie standing where she'd been during the first song. When he couldn't spot her, he told himself not to worry—she'd just moved to get a better view.

The third song was an instrumental featuring the band, and Brig casually strolled toward the wing while he played. "Anybody seen a cute little blond lady in a blue dress?" he called to the bystanders.

"She left," someone mouthed, and pointed toward backstage.

Frowning, Brig returned to center stage. There must be a good explanation—besides, Kitty was with her. Unless she was menaced by Godzilla or an army battalion, Kitty O'Conner could protect her.

Brig got through the fourth song, though his concentration was shot. As he doggedly hung onto the last word of the lyrics, he looked offstage. Kitty stood there, talking full tilt to an agitated security guard.

"G'night, folks, and God bless," Brig abruptly told the packed auditorium. Then he walked to one of the band members and thrust the guitar into his startled hands. "Play somethin'," he ordered, and ran for the wings.

"Where is she?" he demanded as soon as he reached Kitty.

"I don't think she's in the building anymore," the huge bodyguard explained gruffly. He told Brig how they'd gotten separated. "Dammit, Mr. McKay, she just went to the dressing room. I wouldn't have let her go alone, but that area's under tight security."

"She must have left through a back exit," the guard interjected. He eyed Brig grimly. "I checked your dressing room. Mr. McKay, somebody left drugs there."

After a stunned second, Brig grabbed the guard by the shirt. "It's a plant. Call the police. O'Conner, you stay here."

"Where are you going?" Kitty asked.

"To follow Melisande." His stomach churning, his fists clenched, Brig ran toward an exit.

The night air was muggy, but it felt cool against her

heated complexion. "Drop the phone. You're under arrest."

Shocked, boxer-face twisted away from the sidewalk pay phone and gaped at her. Millie could imagine his amazement at being confronted by a sweaty, small, elegantly dressed woman with no shoes and ripped hose.

"What the hell?"

"I saw what you did in Brig McKay's dressing room. You're under arrest. This is a citizen's arrest, but I'm a law officer from Florida. So don't try anything. You have the right—"

"You didn't see squat," boxer-face retorted, his face compressed in anger. "Leave me alone." He reached for the phone again.

"Don't touch it."

"Mind your own business."

"You're under arrest!"

Cursing, he slung the phone down and started toward her, popping his knuckles. "Back off, you goofy little broad."

"I warned you." Her fist flashed out.

Boxer-face grabbed his midsection and took two uncertain steps back, while pain drew the color out of his face. "Unbelievable." He gasped. Then he turned and half-ran, half-shuffled toward an alley.

Millie looked around desperately and spotted an older couple who'd just stepped out of a parking garage. It occurred to her suddenly that she was only a few blocks from the scene of another confrontation, the one in which she'd defended John Franken Hepswood the Fifth. She ignored the fear that history was repeating itself.

"Miss, are you all right?" the elderly man asked.

Millie pointed toward the alley. "Call the police. There's about to be a fight."

Then she followed boxer-face.

Brig headed for the pulsing lights of police cars and

ambulances. *Please, not Melly,* he prayed silently as he shoved through a crowd around the alleyway.

But it was. She lay on a stretcher, her face ashen, her expression so relaxed that he knew she was unconscious. A paramedic was gingerly examining the side of her head.

"Melisande." Brig groaned her name. He fell on his knees beside the stretcher and grabbed her shoulders.

"Get back, pal." A hand latched onto Brig's collar. "Police business. You a friend of the lady's?"

He didn't care about the question. "How bad is she hurt?"

Brig was dimly aware that the paramedic recognized him and spoke his name to the police officer. "Mr. McKay, is she a friend of yours?" the officer repeated.

"How bad is she!" Brig yelled.

"She's got a head injury," the paramedic answered. "She's out cold."

The world was nothing but fear and pain and anger. Brig knew that he was trembling violently, but he didn't care. He looked up at the police officer and asked between gritted teeth, "What bastard did this to her?"

"Over there." A second paramedic hovered around a stocky man who sat limply with his back against one of the alley's brick walls. "I don't know what she did to him before he hit her, but she did a good job."

Blind fury raged through Brig, and he leaped to his feet.

"B-Brig?" The soft, unsteady sound of her voice riveted his attention. Brig quickly knelt beside the stretcher again. Millie's eyes fluttered open, and she gazed at him with woozy adoration.

The breath shattered in his throat. "Melisande," he whispered.

"I think he w-works for H-halford. I s-saw him . . ."

"Sssh, love, sssh."

"Don't let him go. He was in your dressing r-room."

"He's not going anywhere." His voice broke. "Why did you do this, Melly? You promised."

She winced. "Love. I love . . ." Her eyes closed.

"Melisande?" Brig said in a tormented whisper. No answer. "*Melisande.*"

"She's out again," the paramedic told him. "Probably a concussion. But we think she'll be okay."

Seconds later they carried her to the ambulance. Brig climbed inside and sat with his head bowed over hers, tears sliding down his face. Despite every precaution he had taken, she had been hurt. He had never felt so bitter or so defeated.

Millie woke the next morning to find Dinah and Rucker in her hospital room. Her head pounding, she twisted it slowly and looked around. Dinah noticed her and came to the edge of the bed. Rucker followed.

"Where's Brig?" Millie asked worriedly.

"We sent him down to get some breakfast," Rucker soothed. "He didn't sleep at all last night, and he's too stubborn to go back to the hotel."

Millie shut her eyes and tried to remember the past eight hours. Brig hadn't spoken to her very much, but everything she recalled filled her with devotion. "He kept waking me up and making me count his fingers." She forced a smile. "I think I finally tried to bite him."

"What he did is standard procedure when someone has a mild concussion," Dinah noted. "The doctor told him to do it."

"I know." She moved tentatively. "Not too sore." Millie lifted one arm and gazed at the elastic bandage around the wrist. "Just a sprain." She tucked her chin and peered at her flimsy hospital gown. "Scram, Rucker. I'm getting dressed and getting out of here."

His voice was somber. "I wouldn't do that, Millie. You're in hot water with Brig as it is."

Now that sleep had faded from her senses, she realized that Rucker and Dinah looked pensive. The dull anxiety that she'd tried to ignore demanded attention. "I upset him," she acknowledged. "But I had to—"

"He knows why you did it," Dinah assured her. "The guy you caught has admitted that he works for Halford. Brig thinks this incident will clench the FBI's investigation." She paused. "But Millie, you scared Brig, and he thinks you were reckless."

Millie nodded wearily. "I should never have promised to behave."

"That's right," Brig said from the doorway. His voice was grim. "You gave your word, and now I know that it's not worth a damn."

Millie winced inwardly. Concern washed over her as she gazed at him. His face was haggard and heavy beard stubble covered his jaw. Someone had brought him a change of clothes. Gone was the handsome tuxedo, and now he wore boots, jeans, and a wrinkled plaid shirt. She had never seen his blue eyes look so cold.

"I tried not to get into trouble," she protested softly.

"Like hell you tried."

"Come on, Dee," Rucker said diplomatically. "Let's leave these folks to talk. Miss Hunstomper, you're a celebrity." He pointed to a stack of newspapers beside the bed.

"We'll come back later," Dinah told her.

Newspapers. As they left the room, Millie fought a sensation of sick dread. Now she understood one reason why Brig was so angry. She'd made a spectacle of herself, and he was humiliated.

His face was a mask of controlled anger as he walked to her bed. He stopped, looking down at her without any sign of softening.

Millie wanted to cry in apology and hold out her arms to him, but that would only show how weak she was. She'd been taught at an early age to accept responsibility for her actions without asking for leniency. So she pulled herself upright in bed, folded her hands in her lap to hide their trembling, and looked at him stoically.

"I'd do it again, if I had to," she noted.

"I'll never be able to trust you, will I." It wasn't a question.

She nodded. "I can't be trusted when your safety is at stake. I learned that last night."

He cursed viciously, rammed a hand through his hair, and went to the window, where he stood with his back to her, like a fierce statue.

"You didn't care how what you did affected me," he rasped. "Your damned military pride and your independence are more important than keeping your word to me."

"No," she protested in a broken tone. "But I wanted to protect the man I love. Every woman feels that way."

"Every woman doesn't have to prove it the ridiculous way you do."

His words tore at her deepest fear. She was different, and not even he could accept her, even though he'd tried. After several seconds of determined struggling, she got her voice under control. "You knew all along that I wasn't traditional. I warned you."

"Dammit! I don't care if you're untraditional! I *do* care if I can't trust you."

She stiffened as if he'd hit her. Her voice was barely audible. "Last night I tried *so hard* to be what you wanted." Millie looked wretchedly at the pile of newspapers on a chair by the bed. She reached over, picked one up, and scanned the front page. Under the "Inside Stories" column a headline read, SINGER'S DATE BLITZES INTRUDER AT CONCERT. The smaller type beneath it added, *Petite Blond Girlfriend of Brig McKay is Raucous Ex-Marine.*

Ex-marine? They hadn't even gotten her background straight. She sounded like a joke. Worse than that, Brig sounded like a joke. Millie threw the paper on the floor and covered her face with both hands.

"I have to fly to Nashville this afternoon," Brig said bluntly. He turned around and leaned against the window jamb, crossing his arms over his chest. He assessed her without any warmth. "The feds who're workin' the Halford case have ordered me to meet with them."

Millie lowered her hands and nodded. "I'll be all right."

He laughed tonelessly. "That's grand. Just grand." His voice sardonic, he told her, "I know you'll be all right. I don't have to ask. I won't try to take care of you, because it doesn't do any good. You don't listen, and you don't need my help."

Tears filled her eyes and slipped out unheeded. She was dying inside. He was wrong, very wrong. But she'd angered and humiliated him so much that there was no point in arguing. Once he'd been proud of her independent spirit. Now it was obvious that he'd changed his mind.

When she didn't respond to his accusations, he kicked a chair across the room. Breathing harshly, he walked to the door and paused, his face taut with control. "Say it. Just admit that you hate the idea of any man taking care of you, me included."

Millie could see how anxious he was to get away from her. She wanted to curl up in misery and never move again. "Is that so wrong?" she whispered hoarsely.

Brig pounded the door with one fist. He struggled to speak and finally shouted, *"This is one fight I can't win."*

He walked out and slammed the door shut behind him.

Jeopard Surprise, dressed in a sleek black suit, was the last person Brig expected to see crossing the lobby of the Nashville office building. Millie's older brother left a trail of mesmerized women behind, their rapt scrutiny of him almost comical. He never noticed.

Jeopard raised one hand in greeting as Brig stepped out of the lobby elevator.

"You got my message about Melisande," Brig noted. "I didn't know if the navy could track you or Kyle down."

"She's all right?"

"Yeah."

"You don't look too happy."

Brig shrugged. That was an understatement. "Come on, mate, I'll buy you a drink." He frowned, puzzled. "How did you know where to find me today?"

Jeopard's expression was carefully guarded, but a slight smile edged his mouth. "I heard that you had a meeting with the feds."

"Helluva grapevine you navy boys have."

"Hmmm."

Brig and Jeopard traded a slow look. "Whoever you and your brother work for, I'd wager that it's not the navy."

Respect filtered into Jeopard's eyes, but he only said, "That's a wager you might win."

Millie closed her small suitcase and looked around the hotel room, blinking back tears. It was difficult to believe that she and Brig had shared so much love here just three days ago.

"I'm ready to leave," she told Rucker and Dinah.

Rucker took the suitcase, but his scowl continued to indicate how much he disapproved. "It's not right. It's just not right. It's just not."

"Sssh, honey," Dinah warned. "You sound like Mammy in *Gone With the Wind*."

Millie held out her hands in supplication. "I left a message at the desk. When Brig calls, they'll tell him I've gone home." Dinah and Rucker were driving to Florida for a short vacation, and she'd hitched a ride.

"He doesn't want you to go home," Rucker insisted.

Millie closed her eyes, wishing that it were true. "If he wanted me to wait here or come to Nashville, he would have called and told me so."

"But he did call *us*," Dinah reminded her. "Just to ask how you were doing. He's coming back here tomorrow. He's still angry. Give him time."

"Let us put you on a plane to Nashville," Rucker urged.

"If I run after him and beg for forgiveness, he'll feel trapped. I have to show him that I'm strong enough to accept his anger."

Dinah looked at her in amazement. "When you love someone, it's all right to be dependent. He's dependent on you, isn't he?"

Millie gazed back miserably. "It's different for a man. When a man admits that he's vulnerable, it shows how sensitive he is. But when a woman acts vulnerable, a man is likely to think that she's weak. I want Brig to realize that I need him because I'm *not* weak."

"I'm confused," Rucker said sardonically.

Millie sighed. "Me too. Let's go."

Brig gave Natty a kiss on the cheek and held the limo door for her. She looked at Millie's cottage and the surrounding forest with a slow, wistful appraisal. "Brig honey, I'm going to miss this place. It's about the most romantic spot in the world."

When she saw the stricken look on his face, she patted his arm and added hurriedly, "I'm so sorry you missed seeing Millie. I swear she left with y'all's friends not more than an hour before you got here. It was a quick decision, you know—she got here, looked around, and just said. 'I see Brig everywhere I look,' so they told her to come with them to their house in Key West."

"I'm all right, Natty. Get in the car, or you'll miss your flight."

"Bye, honey. Go on down to the coast and drag that girl back."

"She doesn't want to come back."

Natty exhaled in exasperation. "Mercy, men are so dense! Women like to be pursued, don't you know that!"

"Not Millie. She's different."

Natty settled in the limousine and smiled smuggly. "Don't bet on it."

After Natty's departure, Brig walked into the cottage and stood with his hands on his hips. The silence was unnerving. The loneliness inside him accentuated it.

"You little fighter," he muttered. "You're just tryin' to make me more miserable than I already am."

But in his heart he knew that wasn't the reason she hadn't waited in Birmingham. Brig sat down on her couch and wearily rubbed his temples. He wanted to kick himself every time he replayed the things he'd said to her at the hospital. They might have been true, but he shouldn't have taken his grief out on her when she lay in bed looking battered and helpless.

He'd made her feel like some sort of freak. He had seen the humiliation in her eyes. Despite all the times he'd insisted that he loved her just the way she was, he had raged at her. In a sense, they had both broken promises.

Whether she needed him or not, whether she'd gone against her word or not, he loved her and was proud of her heroics in Birmingham. His love and pride had been buried under layers of shock, he realized now, and he'd been furious that she'd scared him so badly. In revenge, he'd accomplished what no other man in the world could—he'd sent her into full retreat.

The fragrance of jasmine came to him suddenly. Brig knew there were jasmine vines outside the cottage, but he also remembered that Melisande St. Serpris had written that she always wore jasmine, her favorite perfume. He chuckled dryly. "Well, Melisande, glad you came to visit me. What should I do about your great-great-great-granddaughter?"

Her photocopied diary lay on the coffee table. Brig picked it up and thumbed idly through the pages. " 'Jacques finally understood that I could give him strength, pride and a spirit to equal his own,' " Brig read. " 'Those very qualities, which caused us such annoyance with each other, eventually became the things we shared most. We spent the early days of our courtship, if one could call those seafaring adventures by such a civilized name, struggling to learn which of us held the most power. To our great relief, we finally agreed that it was unimportant. He had kidnapped me, but I had captured him.' "

Still reading the diary, Brig walked outside. "*Strewth!*" he said suddenly, and slapped the manuscript closed. "I've got it!" He started back to the house. His attention was diverted by the delicate greenery of a jasmine plant growing by the edge of the porch.

Brig walked over and studied it carefully. It bore no flowers, and when he inhaled, he smelled nothing but hot summer air.

"How about that, Granny Melisande," he said softly. "Thanks for the help."

Millie rested her arms on the porch railing and watched sunlight shimmer on the ocean. Key West, land of Hemingway and aging hippies, was a wind-swept paradise for castaways. She felt morosely at home.

Dinah walked out onto the porch and settled into a rocking chair. "The Coast Guard could use you," Dinah noted. "To replace surveillance ships and radar."

Smiling pensively, Millie leaned back in her chair and sighed. "I guess I've spent a lot of time sitting here during the past two days."

"Hmmm. Rucker says if he put a lantern in your hand he'd turn you into a lighthouse."

"A very *short* lighthouse."

"Why don't you go for a walk on the beach?"

Millie nodded, then stood up and stretched. "Want to come along?"

"No, Rucker's taking a nap, and I might join him."

Millie immediately sensed that her absence would be welcomed. The house was charming, but the floors creaked with every footstep and the walls might as well have been made of paper. "I'll take a *long* walk," she offered.

Dinah smiled. "Smart girl."

Millie slipped her hands into the oversized pockets of her blue-striped sundress and started to walk to Key West's only real beach, a man-made one. When she finally reached the brownish sand strip, she walked down to the surf and let the cool, foamy water rush up to her ankles.

What was Brig doing now, and what did he think of her decision to avoid him? She wanted to give him an easy way out. No regrets, no long good-byes, just a clean break. Men liked things that way.

She had thought that this way would be less painful for her too. But she was wrong. Neither her pride nor her noble resolutions could quiet the tormenting inner voice that said she'd never find another man like Brig.

Sometimes the urge to see him was almost more than she could bear. She wanted to swear to him that she could change, that she would change. She'd become a shorter version of Natty Brannigan—Natty was tough and shrewd, but she hid those qualities under a beguiling facade of helplessness.

But Millie glumly acknowledged that she'd be deceiving both herself and Brig if she acted like Natty, and Brig was too savvy to be deceived for very long. Disappointment would turn into new anger, and that would slowly destroy what was left of the wonderful bond between them.

She let the tears come and walked faster, barely seeing the tiny seashells and white sand that passed beneath her feet. For several minutes she forced herself to imagine the worst possible scenario for her future. Alone, lonely, an outsider. Her brother's raucous teasing would become gentle as their respect turned to concern. Just as Brig had once predicted.

So be it. Brig was the only man she wanted, and for a brief time she'd had him. The memories would have to be enough. Swallowing hard and gulping back more tears, Millie scrubbed a hand across her eyes as she trudged along. She glanced out at the ocean and halted, astonished.

Only a few hundred yards offshore, a nineteenth century sailing ship rode the ocean like a magnificent ghost.

It was a classic reproduction, not a ghost ship, she realized after a second. It resembled one of the ships that had sailed into New York harbor during the Statue of Liberty celebrations. Her dull reverie disappeared temporarily as she studied the graceful schooner. Wind ruffled the sails on its two tall masts, and she could see crew members moving about on deck.

Millie sat down and watched the beautiful ship for nearly an hour. Feeling charmed and oddly at peace, she went back to the house.

"I'm back," Millie called diplomatically, as she walked down a cool, dark hallway to the kitchen. She heard the sound of the upstairs shower and decided she'd timed her walk well. Sighing with envy, she got a soft drink from the refrigerator and reached into a cabinet for a glass.

The front screened door slapped open as if it were being torn from its hinges. Millie swung around, her heart jumping, and stared down the hallway in utter shock as four sword-bearing pirates burst into the house.

Pirates?

They were barechested, though wide crossbelts were slung across their shoulders. They wore only loose knee britches and rough leather shoes in the style of moccasins. Two of them had bright bandanas tied around their heads. One carried a coarse blue blanket.

"Be you Melisande?" the leader said in a hearty English accent.

The situation was so absurd that she blurted back, "Aye. And who be you, you scurvy sea dog?"

"No back talk. Cap'n McKay *said* you'd try a man's patience!" He gestured for his companions to come forward. "Let's go, men!"

Millie was so stunned at the name, *Cap'n McKay*, that she didn't react quickly enough when they pounced on her. She tried to dodge, but they threw the blue blanket around her body and pulled it snug, pinning her arms down. Two of the men picked her up.

"Caught like a fish in a net!" the lead pirate chortled. "Go quiet, wench."

"Like hell I will!" Kicking, wiggling, she fought them all the way down the hall. Millie flung her head back and saw Dinah and Rucker, both wearing robes, watching her from the top of the stairs. Dinah looked uncertain, but Rucker looked grandly amused. "Dinah! Rucker! What is this all about?"

"It was Brig's idea," Dinah told her.

The lead pirate waved his sword at Rucker menacingly. "Give us the wench's belongings."

Rucker reached down, picked up her already-packed suitcase, and tossed it to the man. "Have fun, Miss Hunstomper," he drawled cheerfully.

Speechless, Millie quit fighting and lay still, squinting in the bright afternoon sun as the men carried her to the beach. Once there, they put her in a small rowboat, climbed in, and started toward the schooner.

"Where are you from?" Millie demanded. "Did Brig rent you?"

"Quiet, wench."

"I want some answers!"

Instead she got a bandana stuffed in her mouth. Mumbling darkly around the improvised silencer, Millie drummed her heels on the boat's bottom.

When they reached the schooner one of the bigger pirates balanced her on his shoulder and climbed up a rope ladder to the deck. With the lead pirate following, he carried her below deck and pushed open a small door.

Millie gazed around at a modern galley with an electric stove. They set her on a formica-topped dining table and turned her loose. When they pulled the gag from her mouth she said, "Hmmmph. What are you going to do—threaten me with an egg whisk?"

"Get dressed, wench. I'll be back in ten minutes," the leader ordered. He pointed to a heap of green silk on a nearby chair. After the men left, Millie went to the chair and gathered a gorgeous, floor-length gown into her hands.

"Brig, why are you doing this to me?" she whispered wretchedly. Despite her distress, excitement hummed through her veins. *Kidnapped. She'd been kidnapped. Just like her ancestor.* She didn't understand Brig's plan, but suddenly it didn't matter.

Melisande was going to be more than a match for him.

Eleven

What would a pirate captain do while waiting for a beautiful captive to be brought to his cabin? *Act relaxed*, that's what, Brig decided. He glanced around the sumptuous captain's quarters and picked out a richly upholstered chaise lounge.

He grabbed a pewter goblet full of wine and lay down on his side, propped one elbow on the lounge's rolled headrest and drew one knee up. Perfect.

Someone knocked at the door. Brig cleared his throat. "Bring her in," he ordered in a stern voice.

The heavy wooden door swung open. Brig's chest tightened with longing as Millie stepped inside—or rather, was pushed inside by a burly man. *She's a little princess*, he thought. The people at the costume rental service had warned that the green gown was seductive, but no one had warned that Millie would hypnotize him.

The low-cut neckline and tight bodice showcased her full breasts and small waist. Her arms were extraordinarily graceful in snug sleeves accented by white lace at the wrists. Her hair, curly and disheveled, gave her the appearance of having recently been tumbled in bed. And her eyes were large and vibrant as she glared at him.

"Have fun with her, Cap'n," her escort said drolly.

"Aye. That I will."

The man left, pulling the door shut behind him. Now that she was alone with Brig, Millie clasped her hands in front of her and arched one brow. "I just want you to know that—"

"You've got no say here, woman." Brig tossed back the pewter goblet and swallowed his wine. He got up languidly. "Just do as you're told." His voice became wicked. "I'll tell you when to open your pretty little mouth and what to use it for."

Millie sniffed in disdain but kept quiet—she needed to catch her breath. She was stunned by the sight of Brig. He wore a billowing white shirt with a deep V neck that revealed an inviting swatch of dark hair on his muscular chest. The shirt was tucked into snug, camel-colored knee britches which clung to his thighs and the masculine territory between them. Black leather boots completed the impression that he was a successful pirate captain. Successful and outrageously provocative.

He strolled toward her, his eyes riveted to hers, and she couldn't determine from their expression whether he was angry or amused. He played this amazing part so well. He stopped in front of her, his shirt nearly brushing her bodice.

"This time you can't run from me," he told her smoothly. "You can't escape the way you did in Birmingham."

"Run? I didn't—"

"Be *quiet*. I kidnapped you to teach you a lesson. I'll no more put up with your sass than Jacques would put up with Melisande's. You're here for my pleasure, not to talk."

A confusing mixture of anger and giddy anticipation made her face burn. She trembled with the need to speak, to ask him why he was doing this after the incident in Birmingham. He'd been furious and humiliated. Was this his way of paying her back?

"My tough Melisande," he said in a low, grim voice,

"do you think you can wrap me around your little finger? Do you think you can break your promises to me and then disappear as soon as my back's turned?" His eyes seared her with rebuke. "I won't have it, you hear?"

She couldn't bear to be quiet any longer. He'd provoked all her defensive instincts. "You can't tell me what to do!"

His eyes narrowed coldly. "We'll see about that!" He grabbed her, swung her up into his arms, and strode to a bunk covered with burgundy satin and thick pillows. Millie gasped as he dropped her on the bunk and immediately covered her with his own body. He caught her shoulders and held her still. His lips were nearly touching hers, his fierce eyes so close that she could see silver flecks amid the blue background.

"I'm stronger than you, eh?" he taunted. "Bigger and stronger and a helluva lot better fighter—and don't you ever forget it. You need me to be that way. You want a man who can best you in a fair fight."

"That's the most idiotic thing I've ever heard." She inhaled raggedly, catching the mingled scents of their bodies. His was erotic and purely masculine. "I *know* you're physically stronger than I am."

"I was wrong about you, Melisande. You do want to need me. You want me to protect you. All you have to do is admit it."

"No." She shook her head from side to side. "That's not what love is about."

His breath was harsh as it touched her lips. "You like bein' kidnapped by me, same as Granny Melisande liked bein' kidnapped by old Jacques."

"*No!*"

"The hell you don't," he muttered, and kissed her. He tilted his head and kissed her again, his mouth open, his tongue expert and wanton as it probed between her damp lips.

He arched his body against hers, and the solid, overwhelming presence made her squirm. He pressed the advantage until he lay between her thighs, chaperoned by the silky material of her dress.

Millie whimpered with the knowledge that despite the problems between them, he still wanted her as much as she wanted him—at least in this way. It was a bond, a beginning. She opened her mouth and took the hard thrust of his tongue, met it with her own, and twisted her mouth against his as if she could drink him.

He pulled back, his face ruddy with passion, his eyes hooded, the crook of his mouth showing victory. "Say it," he ordered. "You want to be dependent on me."

Her eyes filled with tears. "I don't want you to dislike me for being weak."

He cursed. "But it's all right for you to protect *me*. It's all right for you to risk your life to take care of *me*. You want me to be dependent on you, but not the other way around, eh?"

Millie blinked in shock. "I suppose I do," she said desperately.

"You want me to be helpless without you."

"No! That's not how I think of it."

"Then what makes it different from you bein' helpless without me?"

"You're confusing me." She writhed under him. "Let me up."

He only levered his body against hers so that she was pinned more effectively. "You can't always get your way, see? You can't always be the toughest or the strongest. You can't always be independent. Sometimes you just have to be plain helpless, Melisande."

She stopped struggling and looked up at him like a cat ready to spit. "I can't be that way."

"You're that way right now, love. Completely helpless. At my mercy."

He bent his head and kissed her neck, tugging the warm skin between his lips. Sensations swirled outward, and she arched her neck with pleasure. Tears stung her eyes at the involuntary way her body strained upwards. "Stop, Brig," she whispered. "Please."

"He lifted his head and gazed down at her. "Is it so bad to be helpless?"

"Yes."

"Do you think I dislike you for being helpless right now?" His voice was strained.

"I don't know what you think," she murmured.

His expression was so intense he almost seemed to be in pain. He reached between them and jerked her skirt upward. Cool air touched her thighs and the region still covered by her white cotton panties. Suddenly she felt his sex through the soft material of his pants, pressing rigidly against her.

"Is this *dislike* I'm showin' you?" he demanded. "Right now we're both helpless. See, Melisande, I'm willing to admit that I need you."

Millie understood finally, and nodded. Her mouth trembled as she fought for control. "But things are different when we're not in bed," she managed.

He shut his eyes, exasperation etched on his face. "*Strewth!* Then we'll get out of bed." Brig vaulted up and pulled her out of the bunk. Her face was deeply flushed, and she gazed at him with torment in her eyes. "Try to explain things to me now," he ordered.

"We're fine together in bed, and you know why," Millie rebuked. "I've never *humiliated* you in bed."

He put his hands on his hips and gave her a bewildered, disgruntled look. "And when have you humiliated me out of bed?"

She blinked in shock. "Birmingham, of course."

Brig frowned. "What are you talkin' about?"

"Oh, Brig, dammit!" she exploded in frustration. "Quit pretending! You didn't want everyone to know that your girlfriend's part commando and part Amazon! I made you a laughing stock!"

"People were impressed. They were laughing with me, not at me. Only trouble was, I wasn't laughing." He paused, studying her shrewdly. "Is that what you think? That I was ashamed of what you did?"

"Yes."

"No."

"What?"

"My God, Melisande, I'm mad as hell and hurt with you, but I'm prouder than ever."

After a stunned moment, she gestured weakly toward him and struggled for words. "You were proud of me? I didn't know. That's why I left you."

"Well, well. Your brother was right."

"My brother?"

He quickly told her about meeting Jeopard in Nashville. "Jep said you kids were taught never to show how bad you hurt. That's when I realized that I'd been too hard on you in the hospital. I thought you were just bein' stubborn."

Looking distressed, she sank to the edge of the bed in a cloud of green silk. Her voice was low and weary. "Then what is this all about, Brig?" She waved around her, indicating his kidnapping ploy.

He chuckled tensely. "To prove that we're in the same boat."

Millie shook her head. "I can't be what you want. I can't promise I won't defend you when you don't want to be defended. The chances I take may upset you. You see that now, don't you?"

He gazed at her while new wrath built inside him. He braced both legs apart, shook clenched fists into the air, and said loudly, "All I see is a woman who's too proud to admit she needs me!"

"Is that the only thing you care about?" Her voice rose and became ferocious. "All right! I can't help myself! I need you!" Shaking, she leaped to her feet. "I need your strength! I need your humor! I need to feel protected sometimes, and you know how to protect me without making me feel incompetent! You're the only man in the world who makes me feel delicate! With you, I can be who I am! But can you deal with that?"

Relief flooded him, chasing away his anger and leaving him drunk with happiness. She gazed at him defensively, and he let her wind down for about five seconds before he smiled calmly. "I'm glad we got your problem settled."

"Nothing's settled!"

"As long as you're willing to admit that you need me, I can deal with anything you do." His tone was cocky.

"I figure that I can calm down your violent ways. It may take me years, but I'll keep workin' on it. And you can work on me. Maybe we'll both get peaceful." He pointed a finger at her in reproach. "But you can't expect me not to get mad when you don't do what I tell you."

"I love you too much to swear that I won't cause trouble if someone threatens you. No more promises."

"Aw, to hell with promises." He sighed grandly and his accent deepened. "I'll take me chances."

"I do need you," she repeated plaintively. "Are you sure you don't mind?"

He laughed then, the sound rich and happy. "*Strewth*, Melly. I'm going to teach you to need me *more*."

"I couldn't possibly need you more than I already do."

His eyes darkened, and his voice became seductive. "Oh, yes, you could."

He stepped forward and put his hands on her waist. The alert set of his body made her think of a primitive male animal cautiously closing in on a female that might need persuasion. The confident, challenging look on his face provoked her to resist. Millie raised her chin and eyed him calmly.

"So you think you can have your way with me, Captain McKay?"

"Anytime I want."

"You may have dragged me aboard your ship, but you'll never force me to make love with you."

A sexy and sinister smile tilted his mouth. "It won't be force, me pretty."

He jerked her close to him and clasped her in his arms. Millie stared up at him through half-shut eyes and shivered with emotion. She hadn't ruined anything between them after all. Brig could accept her as she was, and he wanted her more than ever. "Oh, Captain," she murmured gently. "You're going to compromise me."

Brig molded a hand to the curve of her back and stroked downward to her hips. He grasped her rump suddenly and rubbed, pulling her closer to him as he did. "Compromise. Is that what I'm about to do to you?"

"I've led a sheltered life. I have no idea what you will do with me, Captain."

His eyes were hooded with desire, his breathing a little rough. "I'll show you, m'lady."

He buried his nose in the soft blond hair at her temple, then trailed light kisses down the side of her face. He still cupped her hips with one hand. The other rose to her head and sank into her hair. Pulling her head back, he continued kissing her, letting his mouth follow the curve of her throat. Millie felt her breasts strain against the low-cut gown as she exhaled raggedly.

"That sight tempts my jolly Roger," he said coyly. He bent her back a little further and kissed the soft top curves that spilled over the gown's neckline. Guttural sounds of appreciation rumbled from his throat.

Millie pushed lightly at his shoulders, but his skilled attention had drained her of the energy for much playful resistance. "You *must* stop," she protested in an airy tone.

"I'm the captain here. I can do anything I want with you."

"You shock me, sir."

He raised his head and blew softly on her lips, his breath hot. "I'll shock you more before I'm done."

His mouth covered hers with easy possessiveness, leaving her weak-kneed and hungry. Millie kissed him back with sudden abandon, twisting her mouth into his and darting her tongue along his lips. She pulled back to whisper, "You ake advantage of a lady's baser passions."

"Aye, and I'm good at it too." He brushed his mouth over hers as he picked her up and placed her on the bunk. Brig lay down beside her and caressed her breasts through the gown. "Gets in the way, this dress."

"You're not suggesting that I disrobe!"

"Nah." Smiling devilishly, he reached under her and caught the zipper between his fingers. "I'll do it for you."

With quick, impatient movements he tugged the zipper down. The bodice gaped loosely, allowing his fingers easy access. His eyes gleaming with desire, he pushed the green silk off her shoulders and slowly uncovered her breasts. Millie whimpered with pleasure.

"Well, what have we here?" he asked coyly, while his fingers circled the tight peaks. "Here's evidence, m'lady, that you like a pirate's touch."

She sighed dramatically. "I can't control my willful body."

"Oh? Let me see how willful the rest of it is."

While she clasped at her nakedness and protested firmly, he got on his knees and stripped the gown down her legs.

"Barefoot, are you? And wearin' nothing but panties. A willful body indeed." He removed the panties and continued to kneel beside her, studying her with obvious enjoyment.

"You are no gentleman."

" 'Fraid you're right. No gentleman would do this."

He tangled his fingers in the blond curls between her thighs. Her legs shifted languidly. "No lady would like it so much," he noted with a wicked chuckle. His voice became serious and gruff. "But maybe some ladies are more sensible than others."

Millie looked at him solemnly. She could feel a mist of desire rising on her breasts and stomach. "I'm very sensible, Captain."

He made a growling sound of happiness. "Not frightened by crocodiles, are you?"

She feigned innocence. "Whatever can you mean?"

"This." He stood beside the bed and began undressing himself. The black boots went flying. The shirt was tossed without a second look. His gaze holding hers, Brig slid his knee britches down and kicked them aside.

Hearty appreciation flickered in her eyes. "It hardly looks like a crocodile. And it looks somewhat, well, *lonely.*"

Laughing softly, he lowered himself on top of her and nibbled her breasts. "M'lady, do you have sympathy for it?"

"I'm a tenderhearted woman." She paused, luxuriating in the feel of his strong, hard body pressing hers into the bunk's satin coverlet. "Tell me, pirate, is this what I should do?" She drew her knees up so that her thighs could squeeze his hips.

His voice was throaty, tender. "That's a temptin' way to cure my loneliness."

"Mine too." She touched his face gently, skimming her fingers over the rugged angles, feeling him shudder with restraint. Suddenly the game was over. Happiness caught in the back of her throat, and she gave him a teary smile. "Oh, Brig. Oh, Brig."

The world of love in her voice made him exhale sharply. "You're tryin' me patience."

"No patience necessary."

"Don't move like that, temptress."

"Like that?"

"*Melisande*." After a moment, he said much softer, "Melisande, don't stop."

Much later, he left her napping on the bunk, her hair tossled about her face, and her hands curled under her chin. Brig moved about the cabin, humming under his breath. When he returned to the bunk, he caressed her face tenderly.

She stretched, opened her eyes, and gazed up at him with sleepy devotion. Brig took one of her hands, kissed it, then cupped it over his heart. Her small, lithe fingers stroked his skin reverently.

"Now Melisande, you listen and try to keep an open mind. Will you give up your job and move to Nashville?"

"Sure." She smiled.

He looked at her askance. "No argument? You're givin' me no argument?"

"None. But I'll keep my land and house in Paradise Springs. Maybe Jeopard or Kyle will want to live there someday."

"Fine." Still prepared for conflict, he frowned at her and spoke firmly. "And whatever kind of work you want to do in Nashville, it won't be so dangerous that my hair turns gray."

"If you'll take me along when you tour, I'll have the perfect job."

This was going much too easily. "Of course I'll take you along . . . what job?"

She sighed happily. "Your bodyguard."

"Ah hah. I knew there was a catch."

"I have to keep you out of trouble."

"Woman, you *cause* trouble," he grumbled, but his eyes were amused. "And I'm stuck with you. All right, you'll be my bodyguard." He slipped something over her third finger.

Millie raised her head slowly and stared at the large diamond glittering on her hand. "Pirate booty?"

"I raided Tiffany's." Their eyes met. "Will you marry me, Melisande?"

The expression in her eyes said that she adored him. "Yes, Captain." She wrapped both arms around his neck. Between fervent kisses she repeated, "Oh, yes, Captain. Brig, yes. I love you."

"And I love you, m'lady."

They smiled at each other, and she told him, "You kidnapped me, but I captured you."

"Granny Melisande said the same thing about her and Jacques."

Millie nodded. "A very smart lady." A sheepish expression came over her face. "And Brig?"

He touched his lips to her forehead. "Hmmm?"

"You were right. I've always wanted to be carried off by a pirate." She paused. "Though I never expected him to be an *Australian* pirate."

Brig smiled blithely. "Surprise."

"Where are you taking me?" The devotion in her eyes told him that she didn't much care.

And he gave his answer without hesitating. "Wherever I go, m'lady, for the rest of my life."

Epilogue

Dinah and Rucker watched from the upstairs bedroom as the schooner moved gracefully toward the horizon. Slanting afternoon sun illuminated the sails and gave the ship a golden outline.

Dinah sighed with delight. "Since they're leaving, I assume that everything went well."

"I expected it. Brig can talk the ears off a snake. Millie didn't have a chance."

Dinah turned to him and lifted a dark brown brow in mock reproach. "I'll tell Millie that you compared her to a snake."

Smiling, he put his arms around her and kissed the tip of her nose. "I just meant that no woman can resist a smart, sincere, good-lookin' man."

"When I find such a creature, I won't resist him, I assure you."

"Hah. Mean woman."

He drew her close and kissed her hard. She smiled against his mouth and nuzzled his mustache. "I suppose you qualify as irresistible," she whispered. "I love you dearly."

His deep voice was soft with pleasure. "You know, I liked the way you squealed when I licked your ear a while ago."

"I liked the way you licked my ear."

They were still wearing the lightweight robes they'd donned before the "pirates" came to capture Millie. Dinah snuggled her lower body tightly to him. Her eyes gleamed with new desire. "Vacations agree with you, sweetheart."

He laughed throatily. "*You* agree with me."

She hugged him, and he led her back to bed.

Dinah woke up an hour later, giving in to the knot of worry that had lain in her stomach all day. Now that Millie's predicament was solved, she couldn't put the errand off any longer. Rucker held her spoon-style, his back and hips cupping her body while one hand curved possessively over her hip.

Dinah moved away from him carefully then turned over. He had a rough-cut, masculine face that reminded some people of Tom Selleck's, and she smiled at his rumpled, relaxed expression.

She'd never grow tired of looking at him, and she hated the fact that she was about to tell him a small white lie. Her errand was such a ridiculous, innocent thing, a favor to a friend, but technically it was smuggling.

Dinah sighed. Butterfly cocoons. No one cared whether people smuggled butterfly cocoons. She'd just leave the small package at the appointed place and come right back.

She ducked her head and kissed her husband lightly. "Sweetheart, I'm going to run into town. I'll be back in about thirty minutes."

"Hmmm?" His dark auburn lashes fluttered slightly. "Why?"

Dinah winced. "I'm going to buy some milk." And she would too, just to make herself feel less guilty about deceiving him.

"Be careful. Hurry back." He opened his eyes halfway, draped an arm around her neck, and pulled her to him for a sleepy kiss. "Love you."

"Love you too, big guy."

His eyes shut. She moved his arm away and held his

hand for a moment, wishing that she didn't have to leave him even for a short amount of time. All six-feet-three inches of him was sprawled naked amid the rumpled sheets, and she wanted nothing more than to sit there and admire him.

"Bye," she whispered, and forced herself to get up. Dinah pulled a sheet over him, patted his rump, then quickly dressed in a white shorts set. She picked up her purse and slipped sandals onto her feet, then went to the door and stood for a moment in the fading summer light. She watched him sleep, then blew him a kiss and tiptoed away.

Something was wrong. Rucker knew it instantly when he jerked awake. After a second he realized that the room was dark, far darker than the dusk of early evening, and he was alone.

He sat up in bed, jammed a hand through his hair, and tried to think. He was relatively certain that the room had been full of sunlight when Dinah left. Rucker switched on a lamp and grabbed his watch off the nightstand. Nine-thirty. The house was so silent that the ocean sounded eerily close by.

"Dee!" No answer.

She must be downstairs, though the hallway outside the bedroom was completely dark too. Rucker leaped out of bed and reached for the nearest clothing, which happened to be his blue swimtrunks. "Dee!"

He hurriedly pulled the trunks on and ran to the top of the stairs. Dread filled the pit of his stomach. The whole house was dark. "Dee!" he called again louder.

There was an explanation—car trouble, maybe. But the house had a phone, and Dinah would have called him if she'd been delayed. As he ran downstairs, Rucker started telling himself that he was worried over nothing. He went through the house, turning on lights.

He walked out on the front porch to make certain that the car wasn't back. She might have taken a stroll on the beach. But the car was still gone.

The phone rang, and he vaulted back inside. Rucker ran to the old rotary set on the kitchen wall and grabbed the receiver. The police in Key West had found a black Cadillac Seville abandoned on a deserted road. A receipt for the house rent contained Rucker's name. Was the car his?

Rucker braced one elbow against the kitchen wall and held his stomach with his free hand. Fighting nausea, he said that his wife had been driving the car.

The police would send an officer to the house immediately. He heard those words through a haze of sick fear. Rucker hung the phone up and walked outside, off the porch, beyond the light, until at last he stood staring at the dark ocean.

For some reason, he felt compelled to search the black horizon. "Dee where are you?" he whispered.

The distant night wind was all that answered.

THE EDITOR'S CORNER

We have some deliciously heartwarming and richly emotional LOVESWEPTs for you on our holiday menu next month.

Judy Gill plays Santa by giving us **HENNESSEY'S HEAVEN,** LOVESWEPT #294. Heroine Venny Mc-Clure and a tantalizing hunk named Hennessey have such a sizzling attraction for each other that mistletoe wouldn't be able to do its job around them . . . it would just shrivel under their combined heat. Venny has come to her family-owned island to retreat from the world, not to be captivated by the gloriously hand-some and marvelously talented Hennessey. And he knows better than to rush this sweet-faced, sad-eyed woman, but her hungry looks make him too impetuous to hold back. When the world intrudes on their hide-away and the notoriety in her past causes grief, Venny determines to free Hennessey . . . only to discover she has wildly underestimated the power of the love this irresistible man has for her.

Two big presents of love are contained in one pretty package in **LATE NIGHT, RENDEZVOUS,** LOVE-SWEPT #295, by Margaret Malkind. You get not only the utterly delightful love story of Mia Taylor and Boyd Baxter but also that of their wonderfully liberated par-ents. When Boyd first confronts Mia at the library where she works, he almost forgets that his purpose is to enlist her help in getting her mother to cool his father's affections and late-blooming romanticism. She's scarcely able to believe his tales of her "wayward" mother . . . much less the effect he has on her. Soon, teaming up to restrain the older folks, they're taking lessons in love and laughter from them!

Michael Siran is the star twinkling on the top of the brilliantly spangled **CAPTAIN'S PARADISE,** LOVESWEPT #296, by Kay Hooper. Now that tough,

(continued)

fearless man of the sea gets his own true love to last a lifetime. When Robin Stuart is rescued by Michael from the ocean on a dark and dangerous night, she has no way of knowing that it isn't mere coincidence or great good luck that brought him to her aid. Indeed, they are both deeply and desperately involved with bringing the same ruthless man to justice. Before love can blossom for this winning couple, both must face their own demons and find the courage to love. Join Raven Long and friends for another spellbinding romantic adventure as "Hagan Strikes Again!"

You'll feel as though your stocking were stuffed with bonbons when you read **SWEET MISERY**, LOVESWEPT #297, by Charlotte Hughes. Roxie Norris was a minister's daughter—but certainly no saint! —and she was determined to win her independence from her family. Tyler Sheridan, a self-made man as successful as he was gorgeous, owed her father a big favor and promised to keep an eye on her all summer long. But Tyler hadn't counted on Roxie being a sexy, smart spitfire of a redhead who would turn him on his ear. She is forbidden fruit, yet Tyler yearns to teach her the pleasures of love. How can he fight his feel-ings for Roxie when she so obviously is recklessly, wildly attracted to him? The answer to that question is one sizzling love story!

You'll love to dig into **AT FIRST SIGHT**, LOVESWEPT #298, by Linda Cajio. Angelica Windsor was all fire and ice, a woman who had intrigued and annoyed Dan Roberts since the day they'd met. Conflict was their companion at every meeting, it seemed, espe-cially during one tough business negotiation. When they take a break and find a baby abandoned in Dan's suite, these two sophisticates suddenly have to pull together to protect the helpless infant. Angelica finds that her inhibitions dissolve as her maternal qualities grow . . . and Dan is as enchanted with her as he is

(continued)

filled with anxious yearning to make the delightful new family arrangement last forever. A piece of holiday cake if there ever was one!

There's magic in this gift of love from Kathleen Creighton, **THE SORCERER'S KEEPER**, LOVESWEPT #299. Never has Kathleen written about two more winsome people than brilliant physicist Culley Ward and charming homemaker Elizabeth Resnick. When Culley finds Elizabeth and her angelic little daughter on his doorstep one moonlit night, he thinks he must be dreaming . . . but soon enough the delightful intruders have him wide awake! Elizabeth, hired by Culley's mother to look after him while she's on a cruise, turns out to be everything his heart desires; Culley soon is filling all the empty spaces in Elizabeth's heart. But healing the hurts in their pasts takes a bit of magic and a lot of passionate loving, as you'll discover in reading this wonderfully heartwarming and exciting romance.

It gives me a great deal of pleasure to wish you, for the sixth straight year, a holiday season filled with all the best things in life—peace, prosperity, and the love of family and friends.

Sincerely,

Carolyn Nichols

Carolyn Nichols
Editor
LOVESWEPT
Bantam Books
666 Fifth Avenue
New York, NY 10103

THE DELANEY DYNASTY

Men and women whose loves and passions are so glorious it takes many great romance novels by three bestselling authors to tell their tempestuous stories.

THE SHAMROCK TRINITY

Special Offer
Buy a Bantam Book
for only 50¢.

Now you can have Bantam's catalog filled with hundreds of titles plus take advantage of our unique and exciting bonus book offer. A special offer which gives you the opportunity to purchase a Bantam book for only 50¢. Here's how!

By ordering any five books at the regular price per order, you can also choose any other single book listed (up to a $5.95 value) for just 50¢. Some restrictions do apply, but for further details why not send for Bantam's catalog of titles today!

Just send us your name and address and we will send you a catalog!